Our Literary Lapses
An Anthology

by
The Mariposa Writers' Group

authorHOUSE®

AuthorHouse™
1663 Liberty Drive
Bloomington, IN 47403
www.authorhouse.com
Phone: 1-800-839-8640

First published by AuthorHouse 12/28/2009

ISBN: 978-1-4490-5908-8 (e)
ISBN: 978-1-4490-5906-4 (sc)
ISBN: 978-1-4490-5907-1 (hc)

Printed in the United States of America
Bloomington, Indiana

This book is printed on acid-free paper.

ABOUT THE AUTHOR

The Mariposa Writers' Group was formed in the mid 1990s by a number of people who wanted to write, share skills and information and have an opportunity to hear their work read. Of course, becoming good enough to be published was everyone's secret dream. The first meeting was held at the home of Marilyn Rumball, who is the only remaining member of the original group. The group has grown both in numbers and in activities and meets at the Reception Centre of the Carson Funeral Home in Orillia. For the past five years, the group has sponsored prose and poetry competitions for emerging unpublished writers, held in conjunction with their mini festival – Lake Country Literary Lapses. This festival is held in August at the national historical site, The Stephen Leacock Home and Museum, in Orillia. The day is devoted to morning workshops in prose and poetry, afternoon readings by members and other writers and a gala evening at which the winners of the competitions are announced. With prize money to third place and recognition to fifth, these contests become more popular every year. The Festival has grown since its inception with attendance and participation increasing annually. This anthology, *Our Literary Lapses*, is a new venture for The Mariposa Writers' Group. We hope that you enjoy it.

Members of The Mariposa Writers' Group who have contributed to this anthology are: Marilyn (Cornelius) Rumball, John K. Forrest, Alice de Munnik, Olwen Redwood, Craig Cook, Muriel Hemmings, Harvie Johnstone, Heather Gosein-Leska, Christine Spear, Jim Butler, Joan (Marven) Daulby, Mike Tulp, Elizabeth Bokfi, George Belajac, Sarah Thompson, Barbara Street Brechin and Anne O'Rourke.

TABLE OF CONTENTS

MARILYN (CORNELIUS) RUMBALL

MARILYN was born and raised in Kingston, Ontario, attended school there and graduated from Queen's University with a degree in Psychology, Political & Economic Sciences and English. During her years at Queen's, she was a feature writer for the *Queen's Journal* and Lavana Editor. Following graduation, Marilyn was employed by Atomic Energy of Canada as assistant to the Medical Director, doing research in the medical uses of radioactive isotopes, speech writing and preparing a précis of various medical articles for use in future research.

Marilyn came to Orillia with her husband when he accepted a position with Fahralloy Castings. At the same time, Pete McGarvey hired Marilyn to write continuity (commercials) for Radio Station CFOR. She eventually learned to do a little of everything, including camera work and proofreading for Smith Printing, which was a branch of CFOR for a short time.

When CFOR was sold, Marilyn returned to University for her teaching certificate and began a long career at Park Street Collegiate teaching English, Business Subjects and even Grade 13 Family Studies for several years. She eventually became the Director of the Business Department.

Meanwhile, back on the farm, Marilyn was involved in breeding Canadian Hunters, taking her children to Horse Shows and becoming a Senior Recognized Judge with the Canadian Equestrian Federation (now Equine Canada).

Despite a very busy life, Marilyn still found time to write, but now it is mostly poetry and short stories. She is an active member of the Stephen Leacock Association and Chair of the Student Humorous Short Story Competition. Marilyn is also a founding member of The Mariposa Writers' Group.

If You Build It, They Will Come - Maybe!

It was plain. Orillia had to have a race track. After years of sharing the Lions' Oval with all the local ball teams, Orillia was finally going to have a fairground. And, if one has a fairground, one must have a race track. It used to be that every farmer had a least one Standardbred standing out in the pasture just waiting to be trotted (or paced) out for each fall fair...but that could happen only if you had a track at the fair grounds. So, there was going to be a race track. However, the Orillia Race Committee had even bigger dreams...they envisioned a race season and a facility that would rival Barrie's. And it would all be possible now that the Agricultural Society owned that great big field west of town. The horse community as a whole agreed. My family and I bred Canadian Hunters rather than Standardbreds, but a horse is a horse and if the community wanted a race track, we would help.

Building a race track is not something you just jump into. It takes time and planning, but mostly it takes money. And horse owners, if you ignore the Armstrong Brothers, are mostly broke. The profits from horse breeding always seem to get spread back on the fields. So, how was this race track to become a reality? The Agricultural Society could help a little, but the committee had to find another source of money. We were mainly farm families, and when a farm community needs to raise money, it holds a dance or a euchre party, or both. It takes a long time to get all the money you need, but you can have a lot of fun doing it.

So we danced! My whole family (mother, father and four children) were already dancing twice a month to raise money for the two riding clubs we belonged to...so what was one more Saturday night and another six loaves of sandwiches. The Race Committee decided on the Jarratt Hall. It was fairly close, fairly cheap, and had a kitchen. Now, a kitchen is very important if you are going to have a dance, because dancing works up a terrible thirst...and food helps you drive home. I can't remember how long we attended these dances, perhaps it was a year, maybe it was longer. But, I do remember that the main organizers were teetotalers and this posed a bit of a problem. Any dance organizer can tell you the bar is the great money maker...without it you would have to dance a great many more Saturday nights to make up the difference. You can't charge for the midnight lunch because that just isn't done. So, what do you do? Well, you do what country folk have been doing for years (some of their city cousins have been doing it too). When the great thirst comes upon you, you just go out to your car for a little fresh air. But you can't go empty handed. You have to take along a little something to mix with the fresh air, a little something you can buy right there at the dance. And of course if the folks in the kitchen want to make a little extra, they'll charge you for the plastic cup to mix your air in. That way, you don't have to dance as long as you thought you would, and the folks who thought your dance was a terrible bore, suddenly decide it's a great place to spend Saturday night.

Finally, it was time! The race track would be ready for the next fall fair if everyone stopped dancing and got to work. First the track had to be designed...my husband was elected for that job because that's the sort of work he did when he wasn't on the farm. Then it had to be laid out. My husband supervised this phase as well. Then the hard work began. The bulldozer arrived and with great skill carved out the track and banked the corners. Whole families arrived to pick stones because the beautiful, flat, grassy field selected for the fair grounds turned out to be the burial ground for everything the glaciers had left behind. Next the track was resurfaced and the fence builders got to work. You can't have a race track without a rail...a rail that has to be painted...another weekend of family togetherness. It took weeks of work and organization, but finally it was done. The workers, all volunteers, even the bulldozer and its driver, looked at what they had wrought and became anxious to try it out.

The great day came! The first race was run! A record time was set! What a track! The race track committee huddled. My husband broke into a sweat! He moved out to re-measure his handy work, praying he hadn't made a mistake calculating the distance. The committee still huddled. Then the sign was given. Dead on! The sigh of relief was heard in Atherley. Orillia had a race track to be reckoned with.

It's amazing what volunteers can accomplish. With hard work and a lot of fun, the Race Committee gave the Orillia Agricultural Society a track that was the envy of all. But where is it you ask? And when do they hold the races it was built for? Well, when you go to ODAS Park, you will see the fastest track in Ontario being used for wreck-um-races (Demolition Derbies some call them) during the fall fair. The rest of the time? I guess it just sits there. Certainly no one uses it, not even Standardbred trainers...they've all gone home and built their own tracks. But you'll have to ask the Fair Board about that.

And what happened to the wonderful plans of the dancers, the builders and the stone pickers? Well, there wasn't enough money to build the stabling required if you are going to run a race card and there just wasn't enough time or energy left to dance up the required amount. For the want of a stall, the horse was lost, I suppose - lost to Barrie and just look at what they've built now! Of course they're missing out on all the fun and fresh air...they have a bar!

Listen

Hear the leaves
As they speak each to each
A shifting kaleidoscope of green
Against heavy gray
Wondering when the rain will come,
Begging the clouds to drop their nourishment
Upon parched roots and wilting leaves,
Entreating the winds to blow away the dust.
All else is silent
Even the birds
Who sit
Patiently waiting
Waiting
Waiting
For rain that does not come

Save Our Planet

Devastation
The polar bear; white against white,
lumbers wraith-like across the horizon
and disappears into the mists of time.

Baby seals so small, so innocent,
little heads crushed and bloody,
unnecessary sacrifice to mortal greed.

Green, productive fields turned black,
planted by man with glass and steel
that proliferate at his convenience.

Forests, old growth, rare growth,
clear cut, burned, bulldozed into oblivion,
oxygen replaced by the miasma of progress.

Ponds, streams, rivers, lakes,
Once clear water seething, deadly,
choked with civilization,
Life's elixir turned poison.

Man, careless, unthinking, self-seeking,
thriftless steward of life on earth, taking, using, abusing
throwing away our planet's chance of survival.

Hope
Dark, warm, nurturing,
Birth-mother of all living things;
When Saddened she cries tears of melting snow
that raise the oceans, flooding the shores;

When angered, she turns against her children
her wrath scorching the land,
whirling the winds, destroying her creation.
But always she hopes they will see the devastation
and, knowing their carelessness and greed
has caused her such pain,
they will rise up, cry out for change, but above all act
before it is too late to save her,
Our plant, Our Mother Earth.

Resolution

White arms whirling overhead,
driven by the winds
they create for us
with ancient technology, powering us into the future.

Huge, beautiful buildings
surrounded by green, edged with flowers
hiding the fires within
consuming that which seeped like festering sores
Into our water, into our land, into our homes.

Silence in motion, powered by the sun
we move forward as never before
without contaminating, without depleting resources,
returning the north to its rightful owners.

The battle is ours to be won!
With intelligence, foresight and strength of conviction
we can change our world
we can save our planet!

The Many Faces of the Knight in Shining Armour

Who is that Knight in Shining Armour? Any little girl who has ever read a Fairy Tale knows him. He's the tall blonde with curly hair and blue eyes who appears on almost every page of her storybooks. Well, every page except for the ones showing the evil stepmother or the ogre. He comes to save Sleeping Beauty from napping away her life in a briar patch. He dances Cinderella right out of her glass slippers and he is the avatar of Beauty's Beast, transformed by the love of a good woman. And, just in the nick of time too! A few minutes later and the rose would have wilted and died, condemning him to a loveless life with a terrible hairdo. He shows up again in "The Princess Bride," still blonde, but this time tugging his forelock and saying "as you wish." each time the princess speaks.

Shining Armour is the dream of every young girl's life. Often he is a prince, sometimes he's a toad, waiting to become a prince, and sometimes he's a servant who would be a prince if they would just let him take his proper station in life. He bows and scrapes, rides a white stallion, dances a mean *gavotte*, but in a pinch he's the one you want there to save you. He can fight with a sword, his fists, his witty words and he always wins. And his kisses – ah what kisses. They can wake up the dead; they can breathe "happiness ever after" into every fluttering female heart.

Our little girl spends her young life dreaming of when her prince will come. She looks for him in her classroom, in church, even at Sunday School picnics, but when she thinks she's found him, he isn't interested. And so she waits.

Strangely, as time passes, Shining Armour seems to change. His hair is no longer blonde, maybe not even curly. It is dark, long and often hangs over eyes that are still blue, but eagle sharp. There is even the glint of something shiny dangling from his eyebrow. Maybe his lower lip has a strange sharp attachment, guaranteed to wake up the dead if he is the kissing type. He doesn't sport the six-pack of superman – ugh! Who would be interested in a muscle-bound, high-flyer who can't krump. Shining Armour plays guitar, gyrates like a whirling dervish and in truth is the sort of person her mother has always warned her about. Better not take that one home. He probably wouldn't go anyway; he thinks families are for nerds. Not to worry Mother, turns out he doesn't like girls anyway. He's in love with his guitar.

Time passes. Our little girl is now a young lady. Shining Armour has morphed again. He is still tall and dark, but the body piercings have disappeared. His eyes may have turned to brown and he might even be wearing glasses. The guitar has been replaced with a briefcase. But he is kind and gentle. He opens doors for her, doesn't toot his horn when he arrives for a date, and walks her to her door when they return home. Young Lady's parents love him and he calls them Mum and Dad. She just knows she and Shining Armour will live happily ever after.

Once into the "ever after," Shining Armour exchanges his briefcase for a black bag. He may still be tall, but he might be short and fat. He is dressed from head to foot in unstylish green. Tommy Hilfiger wouldn't approve of him at all. No matter, he is the only man she wants around her. His gentle voice reassures her, his hands that touch and probe give her confidence. He asks her to work with him and she is delighted to do his bidding. When the going gets tough, he is there for her with something to ease her pain. He is truly a prince of a fellow who presents her with a gift more precious than gold. Who is this masked man, this Shining Armour whom she will love forever? Her obstetrician of course! The most important Shining Armour in a Young Lady's life. The Shining Armour who will remain forever unchanged in her imagination.

JOHN K. FORREST

JOHN retired after 34 years as an educator and began writing about the exceptional events and wonderful people that have enriched his life. Drawing on these experiences, he strives to recreate the emotion and impact of those special moments in life that touch us all. His short stories have been published in the magazines, *Reminisce* and *Good Old Days, Capper's, New Moon Network*, the syndicated newspaper feature, *The Front Porch*, and in the anthologies: *Chicken Soup for the Soul (Christmas 2007 and Fathers and Sons 2008)*; *My Teacher Is My Hero* (FW Publications, 2008) and *A Cup of Comfort For Inspiration* (Adams Media, 2003). His works have also aired on CBC Radio One's *First Person Singular* and won first place in competitions held by: *The Toronto Sun, The Packet & Times* and *The Owen Sound Sun Times*. His first book: *Angels Stars and Trees - Tales of Christmas Magic* (Your Scrivener Press, 2007), an anthology of Christmas stories, was released to excellent reviews and a second edition is pending. John lives in Severn Township near Orillia, Ontario, with his wife Carol, where they enjoy golf, travel and follow the life adventures of their grown children Rob and Dana.

Mission Accomplished

As I strode purposefully toward the display of greeting cards, I contemplated the importance of my mission, carefully weighing the risks against the rewards. Under the pretence of making a selection, I began my reconnaissance. The signs suspended from the store's ceiling were of little help. Women's Needs; well, maybe. Men's Needs; more likely. Baby's Needs; decidedly not! Then I spotted it: Family Planning!

My wife had recently given birth to our second and final child and we were anxious to resume conjugal relations. However, pending a surgical solution to my potency, it had been decided that some mechanical means of birth control must be employed. Now, purchasing condoms should not have been a problem for a sophisticated man of the times! But, when you're a public school Principal in a small town, desire must often be tempered with discretion. I was no neophyte. As a teenager I had obtained the requisite "safe" for my wallet from one of the guys, old and bold enough to face the neighbourhood druggist. As a young husband, I had acquired such items surreptitiously, directly from the Pharmacist. But with the advent of birth control pills, followed by our desire to actually have children; it had been years since my last purchase of recreational latex.

Nowadays, such items are advertised on T.V. and actually sold in schools! Times may have changed; but my inhibitions hadn't. I was approaching this delicate mission with all the stealth of an infiltrator.

Tugging my Tilly™ hat lower on my forehead, I started to saunter nonchalantly toward my goal. The aisle was empty of people but the in-store Muzak™ grated on my frayed nerves. Alone and unobserved, I came to a halt directly under the overhead sign and let my eyes fall casually on to the display.

My God! There were thousands of them! I was stunned by this vast array and the unexpected complexity of my task. Multicoloured boxes of prophylactics were stacked and racked for my personal perusal. They were divided by brand name and subdivided by thickness, lubrication and other special features; even colour and size! Which should I choose? What size do I take and should I base my choice on ego or reality? For all I knew they had a fitting room!

Mesmerised, I began to study the packaging; not yet daring to actually touch a box. I was reaching tentatively for one emblazoned with the head of some ancient warrior, when I detected a presence at my side.

"May I help you sir?" piped the young Pharmacist's Assistant.

I snatched my hand back. "Thank you, no." I replied. "Just looking!"

"Oh hello Mr. Forrest! I didn't recognize you at first, but I would never forget that voice. It's been ten years since I graduated. Do you remember me?"

"Why, yes, Shelley, I do." I replied, rather more heartily than necessary. Caught in the act, there was nothing to do but brazen it out. As we stood there exchanging pleasantries, I shifted my weight nervously from foot to foot much like a child needing to go to the bathroom. Finally, after what seemed an eternity, my former student reached up, selected a package from the shelf and placed it in my hand.

"Here," she said, "try these. My husband and I use them and they're on special today. It was nice seeing you again!" Off she went.

I glanced furtively at the box in my hand, palmed it out of sight and set off toward the checkout. I approached the front of the store cautiously. There were two cashiers. Thankfully neither of them looked familiar to me. I took up a position near the battery display and waited for an opening. It came!

I made my move and slipped into line, just as a clerk was bagging the preceding customer's items. For camouflage, I grabbed a newspaper from the rack, held it over my purchase, and set them both on the counter. While the cashier scanned my merchandise, I carefully scrutinised the lurid headlines on the checkout Tabloids. "Will that be all sir?" she asked.

"Yes thank you." I replied quietly.

She punched in the total, I extended payment and an alarm went off. A red light mounted on the cash register began to flash and a crowd gathered.

"Congratulations sir!" smiled the woman holding my money.

A young man clutching a microphone appeared at my side and repeated the congratulations for the benefit of my fellow shoppers. His voice boomed back at me from the loudspeakers mounted throughout the store.

"Well shoppers, if you've been following our promotion today, you know that the 1000th customer has just stepped through the checkout. And his name is..." He broke off and shoved the microphone under my nose. I froze. Dead air followed. The announcer quickly went on. "He's speechless ladies and gentlemen. Overwhelmed perhaps, by his good fortune in winning a year's supply of his purchase today. Now let's see what he's won!"

He reached for the small package sitting atop my paper.

I snapped! A man can only take so much! Snatching up both items, I bolted for the exit. The stunned crowd parted like the Red Sea as I shouldered my way through.

"Your change sir!" cried the cashier.

"Your prize sir!" called the Disk Jockey.

"Keep it!" I bellowed in my wake, as I charged out the door.

Stumbling onto the sunlit sidewalk; I thrust my precious package deep in my pocket, straightened my hat, tucked the paper under my arm and walked briskly to my car.

As I drove out of the lot the tension drained from my neck and shoulders, replaced by an aura of relief and accomplishment. Someone else could have a year's supply of diapers, deodorant or dental floss; I had gotten what I'd come for!

And, after all; I only needed enough to last until my vasectomy. But that is another story.

Rite Of Passage

The sun was beginning to set over the sparkling waters of Lake Eugenia, heralding the final few hours of my fishing trip with my son. So far it had been a disaster. Everything had gone wrong! We had snagged our propeller, tangled tackle, lost lures and punctured a hole in our inflatable boat. It had teemed rain, been miserably cold and chipmunks had gnawed their way into our food box and munched on our marshmallows. But worst of all, we had not yet caught a single fish!

You see, a long line of our family's fathers had taken their sons on fishing trips, to mark their coming of age. Each generation had its story to tell. This was our special trip and today had been our last chance to write a tale of our own.

Our misadventures began, after my nine-year old, Rob, coerced me into taking him on a fishing trip. Now you must understand that, contrary to family genealogy, I have a decidedly limited enthusiasm for outdoor activity. Walks on a nearby nature trail, weekends at a friend's cottage and fishing for perch off the dock, highlight the extent of my wilderness experience. The blood of the *Courier de Bois* does not run in my veins! Rob, however, must have been a throwback. He was tenacious in his quest for an outdoor adventure with his Dad and, finally, after some caustic comments about role modelling and male bonding, I was forced to rise to the challenge. Or more aptly put, I ran out of excuses! Would my fatherhood stand the test?

After much discussion, examination of maps, and reference to fishing guides and the solunar tables in the *Toronto Star* (I always wondered what they were for!), we decided on a two-day safari to Lake Eugenia; a hydro reservoir, which sits perched above the Beaver Valley near the frontier town of Flesherton in darkest Central Ontario. The fact that our destination was just a ten-minute drive from the security of Grandma's house had some bearing on my choice!

Given our lack of experience and basic equipment, planning for the trip was a major undertaking. In fact, I'm certain the Allies put less effort into launching their assault on the beaches of Normandy than we did into preparing for our encounter with the elements!

We made lists and more lists: clothing, cooking utensils, food, accessories, an inflatable boat, an electric motor and, of course, fishing tackle. We begged and borrowed what we could and spent enough money on shopping trips to various outfitters and food stores, to ensure the local merchants a successful summer. Our basement staging area took on the appearance of a base camp for an assault on Mount Everest. On the eve of the trip, the atmosphere was tense with anticipation. We packed the truck and set our alarms. We could hardly sleep, as visions of *voyageurs* and images of trophy bass crowded our dreams.

We were off at the crack of dawn. Thanks to my flawless navigation (an Automobile Association map) and some last-minute directions from a group of helpful hikers out for a morning stroll, we reached our goal. There, before us, lay the pristine waters of Lake Eugenia. The waves were washing gently over the tops of hundreds of partially submerged stumps and thousands of lily pads dotted the surface of the bay. The conditions were exactly those described in our fishing guide and promised to be ideal for harbouring schools of ravenous game fish. You could almost see the bass flicking their fins, daring us to catch them!

We pulled into a beautiful lakeside picnic area! It had all the amenities, including a dock, and most importantly, an outhouse! My chest swelled with pride at this initial success, until Rob tactfully pointed out the sign prohibiting overnight camping.

Somewhat crestfallen, we set off to find a campground. The one we chose was ideal for our initial outdoor experience. In addition to a waterfront campsite, it boasted flush toilets, a snack bar and a heated swimming pool! We unpacked and began to set up.

Things went smoothly as we carefully laid out our camp, constructed our fire ring and selected and levelled the ideal spot for our tent. Borrowed from a friend, our custom made four man double-walled mylar mansion, would provide us with the ultimate in outdoor sleeping comfort and camping convenience. Yes, our tent. I could picture it in my mind. Rolled and tied carefully into its nylon carrying bag, it had been placed strategically in the garage for easy loading. Unfortunately, I could also picture it still sitting there; left behind in the hustle and haste of departure. Time for a conference. How would we deal with our first serious setback? We only briefly considered retreating to Grandma's house for accommodation; but that would be admitting defeat before the battle was even begun. We were made of tougher stuff than that! We did have our sleeping bags and the truck had a cab, so Rob suggested storing our gear outside and sleeping in the back. The quarters would be a little cramped; but a decision was made. We would make do! We emptied the truck and arranged everything in apple pie order creating a model camp. Next, we inflated our boat, mounted the motor and loaded our fishing tackle. We were ready! Thinking it wise to consult with our fellow sportsmen with regard to the current conditions, we strolled the shoreline seeking advice and tips on the honey holes and hot spots. We were only slightly dismayed when we were told that much of Lake Eugenia had been drained over the winter and that the reservoir was only now returning to summer levels. Although the Bass Season had been open for only a couple weeks, catches to date had been poor. Sobered by this less than promising intelligence report, we conferenced again; but, still confident, in our ability to adapt, we decided to persevere.

By now it was past noon and our stomachs were beginning to signal their need for food. To cook or not to cook? Time was marching on and we wanted to get our lines wet. Another conference and we reached a compromise. Just this once, we would take advantage the campground's kitchen.

So, fortified with a hearty shore lunch of burgers and fries from the snack bar, we launched our craft and finally began our assault on the bass.

We made a less than auspicious beginning. The water at our end of the lake was extremely shallow. After launching, we spent most of our time searching for a channel. We fought our way through; dodging stumps, rowing, wading and constantly cleaning our propeller of weeds as we struggled to reach deeper water. Now I know how Humphrey Bogart felt in *The African Queen*; but, eventually, we made it to open water. Then Mother Nature decided to get into the act.

The wind rose, the waves began to crest, our small electric motor laboured and we started to lose way! Undaunted, we unshipped the oars and pressed on. Picture it. Me working the motor and steering, while Rob rowed, as we strove valiantly to get up enough speed to troll our lures as we fought our way back to shore. We limped into camp, chastened and empty handed. I was certain I could hear the sound of fish giggling.

Well, no matter! Dining in the great out of doors would lift our spirits! You can imagine my chagrin when I discovered that, while we were away from our campsite, chipmunks had gnawed a hole in our styrofoam cooler and sampled our supplies! We salvaged what we could and began to prepare our first camp-cooked meal: steak and home fries, seared over an open fire.

A disposable lighter got us off to a good start, but the elements interfered yet again. The wind blew, smoke swirled and our eyes watered. However, regardless of singed eyebrows and second degree burns to our hands and in spite of the fact that our steaks and potatoes were charred on the outside, raw on the inside and seasoned with liberal amounts of fly ash and first-aid ointment; we dined with relish. Revitalized, we got back to fishing. The wind had dropped and we located the channel right away, so the stumps and weeds didn't bother us much this time. Unfortunately, neither did the fish!

Shut out again, we slunk back to camp, toasted a few chipmunk-chewed marshmallows over our campfire and then retreated to the truck to sleep. I dozed off to the sound of waves lapping gently against the shore. Apparently, Rob didn't. He maintains that my staccato-like snoring, not only drowned out the music of the night, but would probably have deterred a rabid wolf. We awoke refreshed at 5:30 a.m., shivered over our cardboard boxes of Kellogg's snack-pack cereal and sallied forth at first light. The fish, however, decided to sleep in. By noon we had had enough and limped back to the dock with empty stringers and literally, that sinking feeling. Not only were our egos deflating, so was our boat! A submerged stump had holed the largest flotation chamber in our rubber raft and we were losing air at an alarming rate. Undaunted, we dug out the patching kit and carried out running repairs. We could cope! And then, the rains came. But by now, we were determined not to let our ancestors down. Donning sou'westers and looking for all the world like Newfie fishermen in a toy boat, we tenaciously struck out again. Damp, but determined, we stuck with it. We stalked our finned quarry around the lake, fishing each likely spot. We plopped plugs near sunken stumps and spun spinners through the weeds. We spent the rest of that day trying every lure in our tackle boxes and testing each technique. We cast; we cranked; we jigged; we baited and we waited; in vain.

Finally, late in the afternoon, the skies cleared. Only a few wispy clouds still floated overhead and the surface of the lake rippled in the light evening breeze. The sun came out, but the fish didn't and our lures still remained untouched. Forsaking camp cooking, we quaffed coke and gnawed on granola bars while continuing our quest for fish; but, eventually, time ran out on us. As the sun began to set, I was forced to turn the boat for home. Rob sat facing me, with shoulders slumped in disappointment, trolling his bait behind, while we concocted exotic and elaborate excuses to explain our lack of success. We were fishing failures!

Our bow approached the dock. I shut down the motor and Rob reluctantly began to retrieve his lure. Suddenly, his line jerked taut and streaked away from the boat. He pulled back to set the hook and a huge large-mouth bass exploded from the lake. The fight was on! Rob's rod bowed as fins and fingers strained in combat. His wily opponent, twisted, turned, leaped and dove, using every trick he knew in his fight for freedom. But the line held and Rob slowly began to gain ground. Then catastrophe struck!

In the midst of this titanic struggle, our temporary patch popped loose and began to hiss angrily as the air gushed from our rubber raft! We were sinking! I sprang into action! Alternating between pumping, panting and shouting enthusiastic, if not expert, instructions! I did my best to keep us afloat. But, it was a losing battle. We were going down fast!

Rob, however, kept his cool, ignored our predicament and played his fish.

As our craft sank slowly to the bottom, that mighty monster broke water time and again, dancing on its tail, trying valiantly to throw the hook. The struggle continued and my heart pounded in my throat as father and son stood side by side, knee deep in water in our sunken craft, working together to land that battling bass.

Then, Rob's line went limp! Time stood still as he reeled furiously, taking up the slack.

Was our quarry still hooked? That question was answered in an instant, by one last leap. Scales of green and gold glistened in the spray as that "bucket-mouth" burst from the water and splashed down right beside us. I scooped and with a cry of triumph, netted our catch.

Shaking with excitement, we abandoned ship and waded to shore, bearing our prize on high. During the struggle some fellow campers had gathered near the dock and their cries of "Way to go kid!" and "Great fish!" filled our ears!

My chest swelled with pride as Rob lifted that "lunker" from the net and strained to hold it aloft. Cameras clicked. Measurements were taken and noted. Then he gently placed that monarch of the lake in the dockside holding tank and we watched in awe as he swam majestically about. Rob and I rescued the boat, dragged it up on shore and began to dry and pack our soggy gear. As we worked together he didn't say much; but when he spoke I could hear a new confidence in the tone of his voice.

That night we sat at our campfire, reliving the battle. Instant celebrities and now seasoned veterans, we dispensed sage angling advice to any and all who stopped by to see The Fish. I still tease Rob that he slept with a smile on his face all night long. I suspect I did too!

Morning came. The truck was loaded. It was time to go; but I knew there was one thing left to do. Rob walked alone out on to the dock, paused for a moment and then carefully tipped the tank spilling the water and returning his fish to its watery lair. Those silver fins flashed for a final time and, as he swam from sight a weary warrior heading home, I said a silent thank you to speed him on his way. Now we all had tales to tell.

A magic moment; a first rite of passage and a special memory, in the lives of both father and son. May we share many more!

ALICE de MUNNIK

ALICE was born in the Netherlands and immigrated to Canada in the early 1950s. She spent her formative years in Orillia and then moved to Toronto. Although she is now semi-retired, Alice's working career included being a legal secretary, trainer and supervisor in large law firms in Toronto and Vancouver, a teaching master at Seneca College, a lecturer at Ryerson University and a life-issues therapist. For the past six years, Alice has taught classes to people who want to write their family stories and has done editing for writers and university students.

Alice started writing as a teenager and has written close to 100 poems, a memoir entitled *Assimilating*, an as yet untitled novel, which is at the revision stage, and a collection of short stories entitled *Dreams and Other Nightmares*. She is currently working on a collection of animal stories. Since 2005, Alice has been the editor of the anthology created by participants in the Orillia Library Lifescapes Programme, as well as an Anthology of the Lifescapes Alumni Group. She is a member of The Mariposa Writers' Group, The Writer's Cauldron writing group and the Lifescapes Alumni Group. Her interests include reading American, Canadian and English fiction, as well as fiction in translation from non-English-speaking countries, social geography, world cultures and psychology.

Elephants I Have Known

For years, the elephant was my personal symbol. It seemed to suit me. I decorated my apartment with them. My first elephants came from India, sold to me by Mohammed, a classmate in my University of Toronto Political Science night class.

I agreed to buy one. "Would you take a family," he asked in his gentle voice when he brought a large box filled with teak elephants to class. "I hate to split them up." So, I bought a mother, a father, a teenager and a child, a mid-life deviation from my usual frugality. I called them my U of T family. I arranged them on the top shelf of my wall unit, where they would have lots of room to roam.

When I came home from work the first day after I got them, the elephants had helped themselves to my library. The father was lying on his belly, trunk down out of the way, as he rested his elbows on either side of my copy of Stephen Leacock's *Sunshine Sketches of a Little Town*. He chuckled out loud at a passage he was reading from "The Sinking of the Mariposa Belle." His wife was on the second shelf of the wall unit, absent-mindedly twirling her trunk, reading *A Room of One's Own*. She looked perplexed. She didn't strike me as the kind to read Virginia Woolf, but, I guess, when it comes to books, there's no accounting for taste is there?

The teenaged elephant was reading "The Little Match Girl" from *The Classic Fairy Tales of Anderson and Grimm*. His little brother was in tears and the story was only half over. "Maybe it's time to stop," I said. "Your little brother is getting very upset."

"He's not my brother, he's my sister," the teenage elephant shot back. "Little girls cry at everything, you should know that. You're a girl."

They all closed the books they were reading and settled down for a nap, while I got their dinners ready. But what was I going to feed them? Mohammed hadn't told me what elephants eat. The father elephant saved me the trouble. He climbed down from the top shelf of the wall unit and walked to where I was in the kitchen.

"Could I speak to you?" he asked softly.

"Yes, of course," I replied.

"Could we discuss the menu for our dinners?"

We sat down at the kitchen table. He lay his trunk on the table and moved closer. "My wife, Margaret, and I only eat once a day at dinner time. We're mostly vegetarian now. Herbie and Flossie eat twice a day. They're still growing as you can see.

"All right," I said, "but what do elephants eat? Are there things that elephants never eat and do you have any favourites?"

"Anything is fine for Margaret and me, other than avocados because they are so high in calories. Also, we'll have whatever vegetable you're having, except for parsnips and turnips. We don't care for either of them."

"Okay. That's fine for you and Margaret, but what about the children?"

"The children..." Just then Margaret lumbered into the kitchen. "The children," will have whatever you're having. They're particularly fond of curries, but when we were traveling through Italy, they also became quite fond of spaghetti and meatballs. Flossie just eats it up and Herbie loves to twirl it around his trunk before he drops it into his mouth."

"Now, we think it is best, that is, Harold and I think it is best that the children eat first and then when they're finished, Harold and I will eat. You could join us if you wish, although you might want to eat on your own."

I glared at Margaret, but she didn't take any notice.

"All right," I said. "How much do elephants eat? I always thought that elephants ate tons of food?"

Margaret blanched and was silent. Harold filled the silence. "Margaret is very sensitive about her weight. She eats very small portions, but as you can see, it does not seem to make a great deal of difference. Isn't that right, dear?"

"Yes, Harold. No matter what I do, I've been 4,200 lbs. since I was a girl and no matter what I eat or don't eat, it all comes out the same. Now, Harold here, he's been 2,000 lbs. since we were married, no matter what he puts in his mouth. He eats what I eat to keep me company and to support me in keeping the pounds off."

"So, how small is a small portion? I mean, are we talking about a bowl, a bucket or what?"

Margaret gasped. Harold looked shocked. "Oh, no, Miss Atkinson, we only dine on the very best china. Margaret always says that food tastes so much better on good bone china than in a plastic bowl. As for buckets, that's only for circus animals. We're from the Royal Court of the Maharaja of Jaipur.

My food bill went sky high. After a while, I had to get a second job as a grocery checker at the local No Frills™ Store to feed my guests and I gave up my university night classes.

Two years after my family settled in, I got Buffy. She was left outside my door one morning. Instead of my morning newspaper, a large wicker basket sat on my rubber welcome mat. I lifted off the flannelette sheet and Buffy smiled up at me. She curtsied and raised her trunk and offered me her front legs. As she didn't come with any clothes, I quickly ran up a couple of pinafores for her on the sewing machine – one in pink and the other in yellow, with matching ribbons for her neck. I did want her to look good.

Buffy was so easy to please. She liked everything, especially the clothes I made her and the books and television programmes I selected. Even her diet was easy. She always ate hay in the morning for fibre and peanuts at night for protein. The only thing that Buffy and I ever fought about was school. Buffy wanted to go to school and I insisted that she stay at home where I could teach her everything she needed to know. After all, wasn't I a school teacher?

"May I speak to you," Margaret asked one day after a particularly difficult day with Buffy, "on a matter of the gravest importance?"

"Sure, as soon as I finish these dishes." It wouldn't hurt Margaret to pitch in once in a while and help with the cleaning up, but I certainly wasn't going to ask. Margaret waited patiently as I lingered over the dishes for as long as I could. "All right, Margaret, what's on your mind?"

"I do wish you'd learn to speak with a little more respect." When I didn't respond, she let it go, but I could tell by the frown on her large forehead that she wasn't pleased with me. "How much experience have you had raising children, Miss Atkinson?"

"Children? None," I answered, "other than the kids I teach."

"I thought so," Margaret said with chagrin, which showed in the creases that circled her eyes. "As an experienced mother, may I offer some advice?"

"Sure, why not?" Margaret bristled at the nonchalance in my voice.

"Buffy is a fragile child and needs a gentle guiding hand. At the same time, she also needs a lot of understanding and love. It wouldn't do you any harm to make her feel special once in a while. Do you understand what I am saying?"

"Sure, I understand, Margaret. You don't think that I'm doing right by Buffy. You think I'm not a good parent, that I don't have the patience or the love a mother should have for her once favourite child."

"Oh, dear. Nothing as drastic as that, surely! I just think that you should allow Buffy to go to school and do some of the things she wants to do, rather than what you want for her. She is a charming and social young elephant. There is much to be said for that."

Was I really such a poor parent? After a few more difficult weeks with Buffy, I finally relented and she went to school with Flossie and Herbie. The first thing Buffy's teacher did was enroll her in dance class – modern jazz mostly. All Buffy wanted to do once she'd finished her homework was dance. And, Bob Fosse! She thinks the sun rises and sets on that man. We've seen every Fosse musical that's been in town.

I don't see much of Buffy anymore. She's rehearsing for her audition in New York next week. She can hardly wait to leave Toronto. I guess that's what kids do. I'm sure it'll be good for her creative development, but it hurts, nonetheless. Luckily, I have other elephants to comfort me, brought to me by friends, by my sisters and by the parents of all those students I teach. They bring me elephants from places like Tanzania, Ireland, Mexico and the Philippines.

If Buffy was my favourite elephant, Baron is definitely the most trying. He was just a tiny elephant really, born wearing a runner's white undershirt with the No. 5 on the front and back and runner's shorts like the athletes wear at the Olympics or so he tells me. And he came with a volleyball stuck to his head. I tried everything, but couldn't budge it.

One day I came home from work to find my living room filled with sand. I walked in on a beach volleyball tournament being played by the young male elephants. They said something about sports being the most important thing in their lives. It was Baron who spearheaded the game.

While the tournament raged on, Margaret rested in her usual place on the second shelf of the wall unit reading W. H. Auden's poetry, occasionally glancing at the game. Baron was arguing with Oscar, the referee, the only one of my elephants who wears a black and white striped jersey. "Was too, inside the line," Baron shouted, as he puffed out his small chest and flexed his biceps, volleyball in hand. "Was not," Oscar trumpeted back. And it went back and forth, "was not" and "was, too" until I couldn't stand it anymore. I told them all to get out. They didn't, of course, but they were pretty angry with me for breaking up their game. "It was the best game I've every played," Baron sobbed. He pouted for days and didn't speak to me for weeks. And he stuck the volleyball back on top of his head.

Ursula and her friend, Beulah, were the last two elephants who came to live at my place. They came via Purolator, sent to me by a couple named Kirk and Kerry King from Kelowna, B.C. Ursula was great for the first few months. Then she and Beulah got like Margaret, obsessed with their weight. They started a fitness programme. Just low-impact aerobics at first; then they moved into high-impact exercises. They got all the other elephants involved, told them they were lazy, no-goods if they didn't join. Even Margaret signed up. I can still hear her counting out her repetitions, breathing heavily and then collapsing in a heap on the sofa after each workout.

Harold wasn't in favour of it. All the time Margaret was spending trying to get her weight down was time he couldn't spend with her. "Besides" he said, "I like her fine just as she is. Why doesn't she understand that? I just want her to remain the full-figured woman I married."

I sent Ursula and Beulah off to see a therapist. They were getting so compulsive about everything. They found out, so they told me as they were packing their things to leave, that I was the problem. They said I didn't understand what elephants really needed to be happy. Apparently, I was not providing them with an environment in which they could thrive. They complained that I never hugged them or praised them when they did positive things. I certainly did try, but I couldn't get my arms around their shoulders. Besides, they never hugged me back. After months of trying, I gave up. Ursula and Beulah are now living at the Y and have signed up to be fitness instructors. Well, good luck to them is all I can say.

Once I had 45 elephants in my apartment, things really got out of hand. The elephants made so much noise, especially when I was trying to sleep, that I seldom got more than 2 hours' sleep at a time. And they constantly loaded me down with their problems from childhood. There were the constant fights. The grey Indian elephants got into arguments with the ebony ones from Africa and the ones from Ireland were constantly reciting Yeats, which the elephants from Thailand didn't like because they were devotees of Kahlil Gibran's works. The Sri Lankan ceremonial elephants felt they were special because they only worked in parades. They got mad at the younger elephants for having no dignity and wanting to play "I spy" and "musical chairs" all the time. The circus elephants wanted to do head stands every evening and the neighbours who lived below me got angry and called the police. I was charged with keeping a common gaming house and with disturbing the peace.

So, you can see what a dilemma I was in. I had to put a stop to it. I had to retire a couple of the older elephants, find good nursing homes for them because they were too old to find work. Many of my other elephants, including Buffy and Baron, found good jobs with movie producers. I am pleased about that. Margaret and her family went back to the palace in India. Mohammed picked them up after she phoned him complaining about the overcrowding and the noise. I found good homes for some of the homelier elephants with people who will love them as dearly as I did once.

It took me a long time to get over being without my elephants. I missed them, especially Buffy. I even missed Margaret. I moped around. I lost weight and pretty much became a hermit.

But, that's all over with now. One day last summer when I had taken the screens out to wash the windows, two of the most beautiful butterflies I have ever seen flew into the open window and landed on my wall unit. The larger one, the one with the iridescent royal blue wings, I've called Esmerelda. The smaller one with the green and yellow wing tips, I've named Annabelle. They appear to like it here and I like having them. I'd like them to stay forever, but, then, forever is a very, very long time, isn't it?

Dancing At Mel Levine's

My friend, Joan, just picked up her brand new, yellow Ford from the dealership. "Where shall we go tonight, girls?" she asks us. Joan, her sister Carol, our friend Elsie and I decide to drive from Orillia to Mel Levine's Place in Honey Harbour and go dancing.

At dances, it's always best to sit at the front. That way, the boys will see us and ask us to dance. Joan and Elsie are tall, slim and pretty. Boys fall all over themselves to ask them to dance. Carol is shorter than her sister and not as pretty. And me, I'm kind of cute, but not cute enough to tempt most boys who go to these dances. I'm still carrying the baby fat that other girls lose at puberty.

For me, this evening might be nothing more than sitting all night while the others dance. Like every other dance I've been to, the girls arrive promptly at 8 o'clock. The boys straggle in later, usually in bunches.

For the first little while, it's fun to just sit and watch. Mel Levine and his band are in fine form and so is his fiddle. Under the table, I tap my feet to the rhythm of "The Tennessee Waltz." I hope someone asks me to dance soon. I'm ready!

The hall is filling up. Carol hasn't been asked to dance and neither have I, so we keep each other company. Joan and Elsie have had some really nice dance partners. They're tall, lean, handsome, have cool ducktails and their shirt collars are turned up like Elvis's. And they know how to dance.

Out of the corner of my eye, I see him. I'm sure he isn't coming to our table, but just in case, I keep him in my sights. He comes straight to my side of the table.

"Would you care to dance?" he asks. I can hardly look at him, I'm so surprised he's here for me and not for Carol.

"Yes. I mean, sure, I'd like to dance," I stutter out.

"Well, that's good," he says.

He takes me by the hand. I like it when boys take you by the hand and lead you onto the dance floor. That way, I won't trip or bang into other dancers already on the floor. It's a slow tune, one by the Everley Brothers called Cathy's Clown. He takes me into his arms. I'm glad he's not one of those boys who clutches me to his chest and squeezes so hard that I can't breathe. He keeps a nice distance. He's not a grabber and doesn't suffer from WHT (wandering hand trouble).

"Do you come here often?" he asks, as we make another circle around the floor.

"No, this is my first time." I really want to say something funny or daring like: "No, only in mating season," or "No, only when my husband lets me out." I don't know if he'll find that funny, so I play it straight.

After our dance, he thanks me and takes me back to my table. Mel Levine and the band are taking a break. I watch as the boy walks back to his table. He has on blue jeans, a plaid shirt and cowboy boots. His hair stands out from his head in a mass of unruly brown curls. He sits down, turns his head toward me and keeps his eyes on my face. He's not good looking, but he's a good dancer and he's polite and not a grabber.

As soon as Mel Levine and his band start up again, the boy is on his feet and comes right over to my table.

"How about this one?" he asks and pulls me out of my chair and onto the dance floor. It's a two-step and I don't know how to do it. The boy expertly leads me around the room and, before I know it, I'm doing the two-step. This is great!

"So, what's your name?" he finally asks.

"Alberta," I say, still not looking at him. It's rude to look a boy straight in the face when he is standing so close.

"That's a nice name. I have an aunt named Alberta."

I smile and don't know what else to say.

"My name is Gerald," he says. "Gerald MacIntosh."

We are both quiet and I let him guide me around the dance floor. I enjoy the music and being in his arms. When the song is over, instead of taking me back to my table, he pulls me over to his side of the room.

"I want you to meet some people. Come on, I'll introduce you."

We stop in front of his table, which is filled with people: old, young, pretty, plain.

"This is my family," he says. Gerald goes around the table and introduces me to his mother and father, his two sisters, his four cousins and several uncles. I smile at each one as they warmly shake my hand. Uncle Walter, the older of the uncles, not only shakes my hand, but holds onto it and lets go only when I pull away.

"Come on, honey," the Mother says. "Have a seat."

"I'll only stay for a minute. I don't want to leave my friend all alone."

"Oh, don't worry about her, she can take care of herself," Gerald's Mother says. "How old are you, honey?"

"Seventeen," I answer.

"Yah, sit down and take a load off your mind," Uncle Walter says. "Stay awhile. We haven't had a big, good-looking girl like you for company in quite a while."

"I really should go. My friend will be looking for me."

Gerald urges me to stay. When he can't convince me, he walks me back to my table. I quickly sit down next to Carol.

Before he leaves, Gerald whispers in my ear. "My Mother wants you to come for supper at our place on Sunday. Can you come?"

I look up at him. "I hardly know you."

"That doesn't matter. I'd like you to come anyway. My whole family would like you to come. They'd be really put out if you don't."

I try to think of something appropriate to say, but all that comes out is: "Why would you and your family ask me to supper when we've just met."

Gerald pauses for a moment. "I guess I should tell you something. My Uncle Walter has his eye on you. He's looking for a new wife. Aunt Hazel died just before Christmas. He's lonely living on his own. He's only 49."

My eyes go round with shock. "I can't. I really can't," is all I can say.

Gerald shrugs, looks disappointed and leaves. I watch as he walks back to his table and his family. They all put their heads together. I wonder if they are talking about me. Uncle Walter raises his head, gives me the once over, spreads out his arms as if he is going to embrace someone and smiles.

As soon as Joan and Elsie come back to our table, I tell them I want to go. I can't stay at Mel Levine's another minute.

"What's the matter?" Elsie asks. "Did something happen?"

"I just want to go. I've had enough."

I run all the way to the car and keep looking behind me to make sure that Uncle Walter isn't following us. When I see that I'm safe, I settle into my seat in the back of the Ford and relax. On the drive back to Orillia, I think about my big night out and know that I'll never go back to Mel Levine's. At least not until Uncle Walter finds himself another wife.

A Long Journey Home

I remember the old Model-T as if it were yesterday
Well past her prime when father bought her
A stately matron, she moved gracefully,
But slowly along the country roads
Taking my brothers and sisters and me to church
Neophytes, pressed together in her back seat
For who knew what we would become
Moth or butterfly?
My prayers were simple then
Dear God, keep Mommy and Daddy safe
I'll be really good if you give me the doll
With the red velvet bonnet for Christmas
The one that sits alone in the window of
McCormick's General Store
And, please, God
Make Daddy be nicer to Mommy
When the old car had to be put to rest
Her body had rusted and she could no longer
Climb the hills to church and into town
I said goodbye to her and my Mother
In the same year. In my grief, I was taken in
By Willard and his sleek Packard
Its cold, gleaming chrome misted over as we
Shared unfeeling moments in the back seat.
My time with Willard and the Packard was
Short-lived as the pull of the City became insistent.
I now rode the overcrowded streetcar that lumbered
And clanged its way through city streets.
After a while, I rode with Jacques in his Ferrari.
We pushed that little car to the limit,
abandoning ourselves to the fast lane.

I hadn't noticed that the soot and dust
Had tarnished my delicate butterfly wings
I was not unhappy to find myself behind the wheel
Of the station wagon that John bought after
Our first child was born. It took my husband to the
Train every morning and our little leaguers to their
Ball games, the dentist and the doctor.
One day, John and I traded in the last of the station
Wagons for a mid-sized car in which our son, Tony,
Took us to the senior citizen's home one rainy November day.
I sit quietly in the back of the black limousine
Waiting for my John to leave me and join the earth
Through veiled eyes I see the old Model-T moving
Slowly down the street beside the cemetery.
The door opens.
Gently, my brothers and sisters urge me inside
I tuck in my tired butterfly wings and nestle in among
Them, happy to be home again in our warm family
cocoon. From her place in the front seat, my Mother
turns around and smiles at me.

OLWEN REDWOOD

OLWEN grew up in Orillia. She loves this community and continues to live and work here. Olwen attended Georgian College and Laurentian University to obtain her RN BScN and has worked as a nurse in the community and at Orillia Soldier's Memorial Hospital for 8 years. Recently (for the past four years) she has worked as a case manager NSMCCAC servicing Alzheimer's clients and their families. Her writing insight has been inspired by personal tragedy, loss, love, as well as the challenges of the clients she serves. Poetry flows from her spirit by the wonderful and not-so-wonderful moments in her life and the many others she encounters in her work. Olwen is currently working on a book of poems to give comfort and inspiration to families who's loved ones have Alzheimer's. She has four wonderful children whose love for, and support of, her writing encourages and delights her. She says that the freedom that writing gives her is a gift that continues to grow. She feels truly blessed.

Tormented Minds

We used to be very content, my husband and I. We've been married for 30 years or maybe 35, it is difficult to keep track. I can't tell you the exact date that our lives turned upside down. You see, I can't remember, that's the problem. My husband has changed into someone I do not know. He is planning to get rid of me. He argues with me. He is up to something. He has a plan and it is no good. John becomes so frustrated with me and I am not sure why? He accuses me of things that are not true. Then I get so cross, I end up in a fury and finish with a good cry. I am so mixed up and afraid. Perhaps he is not really my husband. Is this some cruel trick? We used to have a good life before, before all this happened.

I am no slouch. I started teaching when I was twenty-four years old. I had a wonderful career and loved the kids. Did I tell you we have two grown children? Sorry, I mean three children and they are wonderful. John, my husband loves to have them come around and so do I, but when they visit lately, John goes out. You know I am not sure where he goes. He tells me, but I don't believe him. He used to take me with him. We would go shopping every week, but all that has ended. He tells me he is afraid I will get lost. Can you imagine? Me Ria, lost! For God's sake. He is trying to control me. He insists we get up at a certain time. He makes me breakfast and God help me if I don't eat.

He is always watching me. Please don't find this too peculiar. I can't believe I am saying this but John has hired people to spy on me. At night when I look out the window, I see strangers lurking in the bushes. I close my blinds now, so they cannot watch me. The other night I could hear them singing. John says "you're hearing things." I say poppycock to that! They are out there and damn it they were singing! I don't know who he is anymore. He is checking on me. He takes my things and moves them about. He steals my money and he denies it, day after day. What am I to do? Even my children are in on the charade. They don't know I hear them whispering in the other room. When I walk in everyone is all smiles and the talking stops. I wish someone, anyone, would just listen to me.

It really is better when nobody is home. I can always find something to do like gardening or reading. I do everything. That's not what they will tell you. Apparently, I sit on the couch and sleep the day away. I have always been a healthy person. Lately, though, the doctor tells me I need medication. I don't know what it is for? I am positive I don't need it. Never in my life have I taken a pill, not even for a headache. John runs everything. He is controlling my pills, controlling my life, so he can sneak around and see other women. The pills are making me sick. I can't remember things now. That's the way he wants it. Terrified, I tried tucking them into the side of my mouth but John soon figured it out. Now he checks my mouth, like some sort of horse. It is so humiliating.

I had a dream the other night and it was terribly frightening. I woke up and looked over and John was lying beside me. Well, that is what I thought at first. You see it wasn't him. It was another man who looked just like John. Horrified, I lay there until I could muster the courage to escape. I bolted to the door, made it outside and started to run. John was right behind me.

I was terrified he would catch me. I ran to the neighbours. That's all I remember. John is now telling me it was true! That I actually ran away from him in my nightgown. It was in the middle of the night. Ridiculous! You see, he is trying to make me lose my mind and every day it is becoming worse. Did I tell you that my jewelry is missing now! John told me that I gave it to my daughter. I would have remembered that and he is a liar. He probably gave it to that other woman he is running around with. God, I wish I could figure out what is going on here. My kids don't understand. When I try to talk to them, they politely change the subject. I don't trust them either. They are in it with him and I am on my own now.

Did I mention that damn stove of mine? It never works for me. It works just fine for John. When he is out and I try to cook a simple bowl of soup, it doesn't come on. Why? Why is this happening? My clothes are gone too. The clothes in the closet are hers and I don't know how she got them in there. Where on earth are all my clothes? I was so upset I pulled them onto the floor. It was on Tuesday, I think, some time ago. I screamed for John to get them out of my house, but he calmly hung each one up again. All I could do was cry. The clothes are too big. That's how I know they are not mine and he is trying to make me fit into them. That is why he is always forcing me to eat.

Who can I trust? Who can I talk to? I want to go back to my first home where I lived. Not here in this charlatan's home with this husband who looks like John but is not. I miss him and my life. I want to go back to my real home. Can you help me? This is not me and I can't remember what I used to be or what was before. It is all changed. He is going to leave me and of this I am sure.

God, I love her so, says John. I am becoming so weary. You have no idea what it is like for me, day after day. It is getting worse and she follows me all the time throughout the house. John where are you? John… John, are you there?

She finds me, because I never leave. How could I? I love her. She cannot survive without me. In the beginning it was not so bad. Little things started to happen like missed appointments. She forgot the things she would never have forgotten in the past. Did I tell you Ria was a teacher? She was so organized and brilliant as well as an amazing mother and wife. She hates it when I correct her or try to help her. Ria thinks that there is nothing wrong with her. The mere mention of her infliction and she leaves the room. My doctor tells me that this is just a stage and that hopefully things will improve. Her anger will lessen and she will be calmer. I hold onto this notion, but it has been over a year since her suspicions and rages have taken over the woman I knew as Ria. She hides behind this damn disease.

In the beginning, the pills helped. The kids and I had hope, but after a few months, she became worse. She even gets angry with the children. My Ria would never raise her voice to her children. They visit us and take turns so I can get out for a while. I get a rest and pick up the groceries. Ria used to come with me until that one time when we were out.

I turned my back for a few moments and when I looked back, she was gone. Two hours of pure panic. The security guards and everyone in the mall were looking for Ria. She turned up in the pet store and she didn't remember this at all. Every time I go shopping, she asks me again and again not to leave. She wants me to take her with me. I can't; I'm too afraid of losing her. Funny to hear me say that. Funny to say I am afraid of losing her, when I know she is already gone. She is convinced I am seeing another woman. Can you believe that? Married for 40 years, I love her so much. I have never so much as looked at another woman. I fell in love with her the moment I laid eyes on her. It hurts me deeply. Even though I know it is the disease, it doesn't help. She makes me so frustrated. She won't listen and won't let go of all this suspicion. I admit I become short with her. We argue and inevitably she cries. God, I'm so tired. The doctor tells me there will come a time when I will no longer be able to care for her. She will need to go to a nursing home. Ria would never forgive me. I made a promise to her in the beginning stages of this disease that I would never put her in a home. I promised her, so I will continue to care for my dear wife, till death do us part. If only she would sleep through the night.

The kids are worried about me. They have already lost their mother and they don't want to lose their father, too. I promised her, but I am so tired. That is why I'm here. This can't continue. She will be back any minute. She thinks I am with other women. I told you that, didn't I? What will happen to her? I can't take care of her. If I tell you today I can't continue, how will I ever forgive myself? Will she forgive me? Will she remember how much I tried? How I love her still? I see glimpses of her beauty. She is in there still, somewhere. When she goes to sleep I hold her in my arms. In sleep, we are one, till death do us part. Damn you Alzheimer's!

John held his head in his hands as he cried. I passed him some Kleenex and put my hand on his arm. There was not much I could say. There was nothing to say. This is not the first time I have listened to the torture and torment of love challenged by the ravages of this disease. Now John sits, forced to accept he can no longer care for his wife, his partner whom he promised he would never leave, not knowing that one day he would have to say goodbye. John took the forms and signed each one. "You will take good care of her won't you?

"Of course, it will take some time, but right now you need to ensure that she is safe." I gathered the documents and put them in my bag.

Ria and her children came in and sat down next to John. Ria sat down beside John and he put his arm around her. Ria started to cry, "What did he say? What is going on? Is he going to put me away? I'm not going anywhere, take your lover and leave my house," Ria said as she ran to the door. "I can look after myself, tell him!"

I stood up and took Ria by the hand. We walked down the hall towards the back door. "Everything is going to be okay, Ria. Let's go outside. There is a lovely garden here. I hear you are an expert gardener." "Who told you that? I'm not sure. I do like these flowers, though. They are very lovely. Is John coming back?" "Yes, Ria, he will be back. Right now, though, why don't you sit with June and help her pick some flowers." I walked back to my office then over to the window. The children were helping their father across the parking lot. He looked older, weaker, lost.

They held him close and helped him into the car. I could see his face staring out the window with tears in his eyes and in a few moments they were gone. Ria would not have an easy time getting settled here. She may try to leave, searching for John, longing for her love. He will return and they will be okay. They will never be the same, not better, just different. I never get these stories out of my mind and the look in their eyes. However, we will do our best; the best we can to help them build another life. For now, that is all we can do. One day, perhaps, when there is a cure, these stories will end. Until then, I sit and listen.

Broken in Pieces

Good days, bad days, long days, sad days,
These are the days I live.
My loved one has died, taken in the night,
Helplessly, watching his light slip away,
As I held him in my arms, warm,
Frantically, to save him, he is gone.
I am vacant, I am numb, I am alive.
Shattered now, I want to die.
I cry to whoever is listening,
Please, wake me from this nightmare!
Was it my fate, fortune, and where is my God?
All I know is grief takes hold,
An icy grip bringing me to my knees.
It steals my breath, extinguishing my light.
Now my loved ones hold me tight, watching over me.
My pain is overwhelming, numb, I stagger among the living.
My home, my prison; walls of concrete besiege me,
Flooded by memories, recalling flashes of sorrowful events.
The trees whisper, but I cannot hear them, silence.
I heed my children's voices, unable to mind them,
In my bed, detached, my mother now feeds me.
I cannot stay here, I need to run, but nowhere to go.
The air I breathe chokes me, joy eludes me,
Darkness envelops me.
Nothing anyone can do, helplessly reminded in this pain.
Pleasure, beauty, escape me, I feel only sorrow.
Sleep my simple solace. Peace, dreamless, nothing.
My loved one is gone, why can't you see?
See how shadows have swept over my light.
Families comforting words, deeply caring,
Will never comprehend my missing pieces.

Friends try to bring me back, but I singe in this sorrow.

I cling to my anguish, like I cling to my love's lost vine,

Unable to let go, incapable of moving forward, frozen

So please, do not try to make me laugh,

For laughter feels like a knife that cuts at my heart,

I beg, someone hold my hand, stroke my brow,

Catch my tears and keep me close,

Days, hours, pass in amnesia, gradually

Piece by piece, faint healing, fewer tears,

A small sparkle of light in the darkness.

Amazingly light does not go away.

Again, please do not force my smile, not yet.

I am alive and that is enough, that is all.

Time is wonderful, bringing more light.

I will smile again, laugh again, I will, another day.

His loving spirit is with me now, comforting,

As I was there with him, his last breath in my arms.

Good days, bad days, long days, sad days,

These are the days I live.

Dedicated to Harry Stirk March 2005

Blind Love

On the chair she sits, she has no teeth,
She does not mind, unaware of time.
A few feet away her husband, companion,
Has never seen her face,
A horrible accident left him blind.
A wonderful twist of fate,
Meeting the woman he would marry,
A nurse by trade, they wed.
Caregiver and loving companion,
Living their lives, a wonderful story of life.
Two lovely children born to them,
He has never seen their faces, she was his eyes.
You can feel the connection between them all,
Unseen, unspoken, young couple grows old.
Time passes, frail bodies, altered minds.
The blind man now cares for the wife,
She is stricken, her mind unraveling.
Loving daughter, loving son,
Loving husband
Now struggle
The blind leading the blind.

A Moment in Time

Hands warm, soft and tender,
Loving, giving, sharing
Expressive, strong.
Her three little boys,
Playing in the surf, a joy, a smile,
recognized as Mother's love.
Working hands, comforted her children.
Wartime's difficult choices,
Protecting her little ones as best she could.
The gentle touch, her partner in life,
"Leonard John."
Whom she loved so very much.
Reaches out now to take her hand.
The smell of the lake, the call of the loons,
"Lake Dalrymple."
August walks, lily of the valley fills the room.
Hands in the sand, eyes dancing, she takes off her shoes,
Singing her songs. Laughing, eyes sparkle.
Songs I sing to my children, I now sing to her.
As I sang to my grandmother, she smiled.
"Cold," she softly whispered.
I held my grandmother's hands, hers
warming mine.
As hers grew cold, we sat, hearts pounding,
Breaking, we cried.
I saw the spark that left her eyes, she found peace,
The fear gone, her spirit free,
Hands ever soft, fragile, tender, loving, let go,
Reached out to touch God.
I closed my eyes and saw her face,
Her hands were warm, I felt His grace.

Wonderful joyous light welcoming her home.
She touched us all,
In her own special way.
"We'll miss you, Nan,"
Remembering always,
Her skilled hands, creative, expressive,
Tireless. Each picture created,
Hangs a moment in time for us to share.

The Battle

Miserable mind who tries to trick,
Casting shadows on my light.
You must stop this now!
Your fight continues to cause doubt,
Fear, disbelief and worry.
Anxiety moves in quickly.
Oh so familiar so disturbing,
So controlling, overwhelming.
Move away from me,
No, bring me something that hurts;
I do not deserve this.
Something is wrong here I cry.
Light is warm, welcoming,
Feeling wonderful, joyful.
I am not afraid of tomorrow,
Nor consumed of yesterday,
For they do not exist.
There are no winners or losers
Just life. I will live it now!
Rise up, stand firm as darkness fights its battle
I open my eyes and smile,
My choice, heaven or hell
Here on earth.

CRAIG COOK

CRAIG was born in Niagara Falls, Ontario. He taught elementary school for almost 20 years. Then, he entered the ordained Ministry in the Presbyterian Church of Canada at St. Mark's Presbyterian Church in Orillia. His life-long ministry has been to help people find the joy in their lives. He has always tried to find the humour and fun in the lives God has given us. Craig is married to Mary, his best friend. They have one child, their daughter, Hope. Some of Craig's interests are: reading, writing humour, travel, golf and eating runny butter tarts. In fact, he is a butter-tart gourmand.

Craig has finished a historical novel entitled *Daredevil's Angels* set in the 19th century for the 10-to-13-year-old reader; a collection of short stories about Craig and Mary's experiences as tour leaders of various trips and a memoir piece entitled *Down Under, Where?* about their travels in New Zealand and Australia and other memoir pieces. He is a regular contributor to "The Pastor's Pen" found on the Religion page of The Packet & Times. Craig also helps out at the Orillia Public Library with their ongoing Lifescapes Programme.

Hope Springs Paternal

"Craig, I think my water broke." Mary lowered her very pregnant self onto the bed. She had just returned from a voyage to the bathroom. It was 5 a.m. on a dark and freezing December Sunday.

I jumped out of bed and ran down the hall screaming, "I'll call the fire department and your mother." When I reached the kitchen, I realized I had no idea why I was there. When I returned to our bedroom, Mary had called the doctor. "Perhaps you could slip on some clothes and get the car ready."

"There's an idea," I shouted. I threw on pants and a shirt, grabbed my coat, put on my boots and hurried outside. I jumped into the car and backed out of the driveway. I reached over to take Mary's hand, "Hold on, Angel, I'm going to take this corner on the fly." There was no response. There was no Mary. "Where are you?" I shouted. "Oh my God, I forgot Mary!"

I threw the car into reverse and backed down the street. As I drove into our driveway, Mary stood in our yard with her suitcase. "Did you forget something?" Mary asked as she got into the car.

"No, I was just warming up the car."

I dropped Mary at the hospital entrance while I parked the car. When I entered the hospital, there was no sign of Mary. I walked over to a nursing station. "May I help you," asked a nurse who appeared to be about 80 years old. Her name tag identified her as 'Crumpowitz'.

"Yes, I've lost my wife and we're pregnant."

"What's her name?"

"We're not sure it's a girl," I said.

"No, your wife's name?" the nurse snarled.

"Oh. Ahhh, wait a minute. …. Mary. Yes, it's Mary. Mary Cook."

"She's in room 1219 on the aquamarine line in the Dimwittie Wing. Do you want someone to show you the way?"

"No, thank you. I'm sure I can find my own way." I didn't like the way Crumpowitz talked to me as though I were some little kid. How hard could it be to follow the lines on the floor?

About 20 minutes later, I reached Mary's room. She was lounging in bed without a care in the world. As I held her tiny hand, Mary opened her eyes and said, "Nice you could make it. Where have you been?"

I explained how difficult it was finding a place to park and the poor instructions the nurse gave me. "But I'm here now, so how can I help?"

"Why don't you see if you can tidy up the waiting room," said lovely nurse Crumpowitz as she sauntered into the room.

"Because I'm here to help my wife. I've attended all the pre-naval classes and I know exactly what to do," I said in my most confident voice. This old bat wasn't going to intimidate me.

"Maybe it would be best if you waited in the waiting room, dear," Mary whispered. "You might be able to help reassure some nervous father."

It's hard to argue with such logic. I wandered down to the waiting room. I picked up a newspaper and noticed an article about a tribe of people in the Amazon rainforest that lived entirely on rhubarb. I decided I would just read this one story before I went to help Mary some more.

When I woke up, I noticed several other men sitting and standing around the waiting room. One of the men asked, "Is this your first?"

"Oh heavens no. I've been reading newspapers for as long as I can remember."

"No. Is this your first baby?"

"Oh, yes. It is." I said and added, "It's my wife's first, too. I better get back. My wife is relying on me to help her with this delivery. We're a team. It's been nice meeting you fellows." I walked out into the hall. "Now what's the number of Mary's room?" I thought to myself. "Is it

1402 or 1637? And is it on the fuchsia line or the tapioca? I better ask someone."

I walked along the corridor, turned a corner and came face to face with nurse 'Grump'owitz.

"Are you still wandering around?" she barked.

"I wonder if she's had her rabies shots," I thought.

"While you've been having a nap, your wife has gone into the delivery room." 'Grump'owitz sneered.

"Oh my gosh!" I exclaimed. "Am I too late to help?"

Nurse Crumphead gave me a withering glare as she threw a hospital gown at me. "Put these on. She's in room 2." The creature pointed to a room with a large 2 on the door. "If you hurry, don't get lost and stay awake, you might make it in time."

I put on the gown and rushed into room 2. "I'm here!!" I shouted.

Mary was lying on a table and the doctor was there. He asked, "Who are you?"

"Oh, that's my husband," Mary said.

"Too bad," said the doctor.

"What do you want me to do??" I asked.

"Stay out of my way," The doctor snarled. "If you pass out, I'm stepping over you. I haven't got time for husbands."

"Imagine some husband fainting," I thought. I looked at Mary lying there so serenely. "Do you find it warm in here?" I noticed Mary was perspiring a little. "Shall I get you something to drink? How about a Coke or a beer?"

Mary's face was quite red and she just shook her head. Then I glanced between her legs.

I remember waking up on the floor. I was alone and it was very quiet. I stood up. Slowly, I opened the door and peered out into the hall.

"Where have you been?" yelled darling nurse Grumpface. "Your wife is asking for you. I haven't a clue why. If you think you can stay conscious, follow me."

Nurse Crumb-quits led me to room 1219 on the aquamarine line. There was my darling Mary. Her face beamed as I entered the room. She said, "Oh, Craig, come see our precious angel."

I walked around the bed and was handed a living bundle wrapped up in a blanket. I looked down at the most gorgeous face I have ever seen, our precious daughter, Hope had arrived.

Mary quietly said, "Thanks for all your help. I couldn't have done it without you."

Getting Our Feet Wet

As soon as we got on the bus, I knew we were in trouble. My wife and I were on our way to a travel and leisure show for folks over 60. The affair was very organized. There was even a shuttle service, so old folks didn't need to fight the traffic and drive themselves. But when we got on the bus, I knew we were in trouble. Mary and I were the youngest people on the bus. The average age was about 100. Most of our fellow passengers remembered the story of Noah's Ark because they were on it. There was one elderly woman who sat across from us and was particularly annoying. Actually she lay across from us. She had her feet up on the empty seat next to her so she could recline in luxury all the way out to the show. This was rude enough, but then she proceeded to complain about everything during the trip. She moaned about the traffic (and she wasn't even driving). She even complained about the complaints of the other passengers.

When we arrived at the exhibition we strolled up to the ticket booth. Some young whipper-snapper asked, "Are you two over 60?"

Now normally I would be delighted to be mistaken for being younger than I am, but it annoyed me that this person could not see how mature and wise I appeared. " I'll have you know we are both well past 60," I replied.

Having convinced the ticket person we really belonged, we were allowed to enter the show. The first thing I recall seeing was a display for a retirement community. A lovely young woman was explaining all the amenities. "We have lawn bowling, a putting green and a swimming pool. Each of our units comes equipped with chair glides and elevators. There is round-the-clock nursing care and we have a full time chaplain service." We moved on.

There was a food demonstration. The food person showed us how to purée things like squash, turnips and chicken into a lovely paté for spreading on bread. She said toast at first, but then some fellow mentioned something about his teeth and the lady suggested he could just use bread. There was a general nodding of agreement throughout the crowd, so it must have seemed like good idea. It sounded yummy to me and I was starting to get hungry. We moved on.

Eventually we located the coffin guy. He was showing people different styles. There was your fancy teak with sterling silver handles and satin inlay. It even comes with limo service from your home to the funeral home and then out to the cemetery. The limo has its own bar and TV. I could see how a bereaving family might appreciate those little touches. Then for the budget conscious, there was a little number made from recycled newspaper. On the demonstrator I could still read part of the headline: "Lindbergh crosses Atlantic." It was a nice idea, but the handles looked a little flimsy. Actually they were velcro straps and I wondered how they'd last on a hot day in July. I grabbed some free mints from the bowl that was sitting there and Mary and I moved along.

The exhibition hall was really crowded. Mary was smacked in the ankles by a man in one of those electric scooter things. You would think those things would have horns and before you get to drive one, you should have to pass some kind of test; at least a vision test. The fellow driving this thing was waving a white cane in the air and he was shouting," make way, make way." We moved on.

There was a display of footwear. I looked at some neat shoe inserts. They were foam rubber and I thought they would make a useful gift for my mother. She seems to be getting shorter these days. This booth had some neat pantyhose too. They were made of some new fabric, the same stuff they use to make parachutes. One pair will last the average set of female legs, under normal conditions, about five hours. They seemed quite reasonable. There wasn't a lot of choice in colours though. They had white or black and something called "mushroom." We didn't buy any.

There were people promoting guided tours. One was to see the fall colours in Hamilton. It was only a half day and it was called "Fall in a Steel Town." Another tour that intrigued me was "Fruit Picking in Timmins," but that one wasn't going until January and I wanted to get away before that. I grabbed some more free mints and we moved on.

They even had entertainment. There were some fiddlers from Don Messer's Jubilee. I really liked some of the old favourites they played:

"She'll Be Coming Round the Mountain, Danny Boy" and "Kum Bay Yah." There were some women dancers too. They were wearing huge skirts with hoops under them. Several men nearby had to sit down when the women did those twirly turns and their skirts flew out. It was exciting just being there. I could have sat there and enjoyed the show for minutes, but we had to move along.

Mary and I came to a lady giving a cooking demonstration. I grabbed a chair and sat down. Mary decided she would stand. "Craig, that's the last seat. You took it from that elderly lady."

"It's ok," I said. "She doesn't mind."

"But she was already sitting on it."

Picky, picky. I got up and helped the lady back into her seat. So I had to stand, if you can imagine. Anyway the cooking show was neat. The lady was teaching us how to make a banana soufflé using yoghurt and non-fat shortening. It sounded delicious and some of the people in the audience were clearly enthralled judging from the colour of their cheeks. I think I heard some stomachs rumbling. Mary thought the noise was something else, but I can tell the difference. I was really hungry now. I took a handful of mints and we moved on.

We had seen almost every exhibit and we were anxious to get back on the bus for the thrilling return trip to our car. Mary and I headed for the exit. I took us by the funeral exhibit again and sure enough there were still some mints left. I stocked up for the 15-minute journey back to our car.

Mary and I managed to find our bus. There were three buses and it was really important we got on the correct one or else we might have wound up in Gravenhurst, for God's sake. Travelling can be really difficult if you don't keep your wits about you. Anyway, we arrived back at our car and headed for home. It was a great outing and I have enough mints to see me through the evening.

Egyptian Nightmare

Just recently Mary and I, along with Mary's cousin, Bernie, and his wife had a wonderful trip to Egypt. We saw a lot of fabulous sights: the pyramids, the sphinx, rode camels and even cruised the Nile. Some day I might describe our experiences in more detail and really bore you, but for now I want to tell you about the REAL excitement: our return trip home.

The four of us left Cairo for our flight with Egypt Air to New York City. Once in New York, we would be transferring to Delta Airlines for our short flight to Toronto International Airport while Bernie and his wife would be heading home to Ohio. All went swimmingly until we arrived at JFK Airport in New York around 3:45 Friday afternoon. The weather was pretty crummy, snow mixed with freezing rain and quite cold. We left the plane, did the usual immigration check-in and retrieved our luggage. After passing through customs, we checked our luggage with Egypt Air so they could send it on to Toronto with us on Delta. It was necessary for us to go to another terminal to catch our connecting flights to Toronto and Ohio. So there we were, the four of us, dressed in our best Egyptian clothes ready for a lovely summer day, trudging around in the sleet and the slush with the temperature around a balmy plus 1. We were frozen!

Fortunately it was a short distance to the building where we rode the skytrain over to the next terminal. When the four of us arrived at the proper terminal we found the Delta Airlines section and the place was in total chaos. Hundreds of people were milling around trying to talk to anyone who appeared to know what was happening. Eventually I got in a long line for "Passengers without baggage." Then I spotted a woman at the Delta counter quietly polishing her nails. I went over just to ask if I was in the correct line. Before I could ask her anything, a woman arrived and she shoved a ticket at the Delta employee. The Delta woman looked at the ticket and said, "I'm sorry lady, but your flight to Bucharest has been cancelled."

The tourist looked confused. Since it was pretty clear she didn't understand English, I thought I might help. I flapped my arms, did my best imitation of a jet engine, shook my head and yelled, "Your plane no fly today. Cannn-cellll -ed."

The woman tourist shook her head, banged her ticket on the counter several times, shouted "Bucharest! Bucharest!" and then started crying. I looked at the woman behind the counter, shrugged my shoulders and asked, "Can you please tell me where I should go to get my connecting flight to Toronto?"

"Mister, you ain't going nowhere today. All flights out of here have been cancelled because of the weather."

"Bucharest! Bucharest!"

"Oh shut up." I said as I shoved the other woman out of the way.

I quietly looked at the woman and said very calmly, "WHAT!! Are you sure? When can I get home?"

The Delta woman looked at my ticket, punched something into her computer and said, "The first flight I can get you on won't be until Tuesday."

"TUESDAY! Are you sure? Isn't there something you can do for me earlier than that?"

"Nope. Everything's backed up for the next few days."

"Bucharest, me go Bucharest."

"Well what about our luggage? I checked it with Egypt Air and they were going to have it sent on to Toronto with Delta."

"I'm sorry sir. You'll have to call Delta when you get home; that is if you get home ha, ha, ha, ha and ask them if they've located your luggage."

"Thanks," I said. I snatched our tickets and went to find Mary to tell her the wonderful news. As I left the Delta counter, my other female friend was crying huge tears, mumbling "Bucharest! Bucharest!" and banging her head on the counter.

I found Mary and told her our predicament. Then we found Bernie and his wife and learned their flight to Ohio was cancelled as well. We went to a pay phone and I called the train station. "The first train I can get you on won't be until Monday."

Our attempts to rent a car were just as fruitless. By this time, the four of us were tired, hungry and very frustrated. Then Bernie said, "We have a cousin, Diana, living here, maybe she could help us." So he called her on the phone and she agreed to let us spend the night at her house. We all piled into a taxi and rode into Brooklyn arriving at Diana's house around 9 p.m.

The four of us were so happy to be in a warm, dry place that we grabbed Diana and hugged her and kissed her and jumped up and down in her dining room as we sang "Roll Out the Barrel." After snorting down three pizzas and 12 cups of coffee, we felt more hopeful about our future in New York City.

Bernie and his wife made arrangements to have Diana drive them about 100 miles the next day to where they could rent a car, which they would then drive to Ohio. But what about the poor stranded Canadians?

Mary then was struck with a brilliant idea. She used Diana's phone and called our friend Janice in Stoney Creek. Janice said that her husband, Ben, a long-distance trucker, was in New York and he would be glad to give us a ride as far as Stoney Creek. Eventually we got in touch with Ben and he agreed to the arrangements if we could find him by 7 a.m. when he would be leaving the city. Diana said she knew how to get us to where Ben's truck would be and she would drive us there, but we'd have to be up at 5:30 a.m. After another chorus of "Roll Out the Barrel," we all went off to bed.

Early Saturday morning we were all up and ready to face the next installment of our journey home. The day began before dawn with Diana's car stuck on the street in the snow and ice. We pushed, pulled, shoved, grunted, groaned and shoveled. A city street sander came along and the driver got out and spread about 12 tons of taxpayers' sand and salt under the wheels of Diana's car. After getting her car on the move, it was time to say farewell to Bernie and his wife. We had a great time traveling together, so we all hugged and jumped up and down and sang, "Roll Out the Barrel."

Once on our way, we arrived at the spot where Ben was having his truck unloaded. We were so glad to see a familiar face that we all hugged Ben, jumped up and down and sang, "Roll Out the Barrel." Now we're talking a huge truck here, not some little wimpy pick-up. No, this is one of those trucks with the trailer on the back the length of 12 football fields and with 29 wheels. The cab of this truck is enormous with a bed, TV and a Jacuzzi. After the truck was emptied, Ben climbed into the driver's seat, I rode up front in the co-pilot's seat and Mary climbed onto the bed in the back of the cab.

The ride was pretty uneventful, except for the times when the truck went through a pothole, over a bump or across the top of small cars. Then the people on the two seats, namely Ben and I, would float up off our seats anywhere from one inch to four feet depending upon the severity of the bump. It was a bonus that the ceiling was well padded because my head regularly came into contact with the roof of the cab. I noticed Mary's entire body would often go completely up in the air and land with a thud in some of the strangest places and in some really impressive positions.

Eventually we reached the U.S.- Canadian border. The fellow on duty looked into the truck and seeing Ben and I asked, "Just the two of you?"

"No, there are three of us."

"Where's the third person?"

With this, Mary stuck her head out from the rear of the cab where she was lounging most provocatively, gave the young fellow a wink and said, "I'm along for the ride, too, Big Fella."

The Customs officer stared at Ben and I and then at Mary. He gave Ben and I the "thumbs up" sign and a wink and said, "Off you go, fellows; you too, girlie."

Ben, myself and Good-Time Mary continued on up the highway to Stoney Creek around 6 p.m. Ben drove to the factory where he parked the trailer. Mary and I sadly climbed out of the truck's cab. Our daughter met us and drove us to her home in Toronto where we spent Saturday night. By Sunday afternoon Mary, the Queen of the Truckers, and I were in our own home. It took us longer to get from New York to Orillia than it does to go to the moon.

MURIEL HEMMINGS

MURIEL is the oldest member of The Mariposa Writers' Group. She is a mother of 4, grandmother of 9 and great grandmother of 2. Muriel was the daughter of two school teachers, who instilled in her a love for reading and writing. As a young wife, she got no greater pleasure than going camping with the family and wandering off for a few hours to write stories and poetry. Muriel has had some of her work published including short stories, poetry and craft books. She has often delighted family members by writing a poem to mark a special occasion, such as a wedding or birth of a new baby. For many years Muriel has enjoyed attending an annual writers' conference in London. She also gets great pleasure from being a member of The Mariposa Writers' Group.

Our Alphabet

The letters of our alphabet
Arranged a certain way
Can bring us fame and fortune
When our best thoughts they convey.

That's all the letters Shakespeare used
And Stephen Leacock too.
When from ideas written down
Their masterpieces grew.

The brains and minds God gave us
Can control this alphabet
And form these letters into words
Our readers won't forget.

Just twenty-six small letters
Are gifts for me and you.
When placed in proper order
See what wonders they can do!

People are Like Lemons

Some people are like lemons, which are not your favourite fruit
A lemon may feel worthless when its flavour does not suit
A lemon might get all depressed and think itself a waste
Because we pucker up our lips when sampling its sour taste
But look at bottles, packages that you buy at the store
This lowly lemon is a part of substances galore!
Our cleaning fluids, polishes and scores of things we buy
Contain this fruit. Hey! Grab a fork! I see a lemon pie!
You may like lemon in your tea or in the soap you choose
Its pleasant fragrance you will note in many things you use
Our baking recipes require raw grated lemon zest
But if we leave this flavour out, our cake is not the best
So, like this common sour fruit, some people seem aware
Their personality's not good for other folks to share
They fear nobody cares for them until they flash a smile
And words of comfort to their friends to cheer them for a while
But if you've purchased something
not performing as you thought
You frown and keep complaining: "What a lemon I have got!"
Yes, people are like lemons. Some bring trouble, some give aid
So, let us be the kind of fruit enjoyed in lemonade!

Land of Mystery

Once a silent land was born
Where no melody was heard
But wild wailing of the wind,
Distant call of flying bird.

Lonely land in secret lay
Carpeted with forest green;
Rivers foaming over rocks
Flowed to lakes of rainbow sheen.

Mountains climbed to azure skies;
Buffalo roamed prairie plain;
Beaver, fox, wolf, polar bear
Stealthily marked each domain.

In a semi-circle spread
Rocky, stately, towering shield;
Oceans washed east, west and north
Cod and halibut to yield.

Resting in the dark, hidden caves
Softly did rich soil enfold
Nickel, silver, iron, coal,
Oil, asbestos, copper, gold.

Every day the brilliant sun
Rose and set, but human sounds
Never broke the stillness which
Land of mystery surrounds.

Mountains, forests, lakes and plains
Favoured by Creator's hand
Waited all expectantly
In this silent wonderland.

The Long Hard Trip

From Nova Scotia's dashing waves,
New Brunswick's wooded hills
It traveled through Quebec's terrain
Of fields and daffodils

Then up it went through forestland
Of broad Ontario
Across to Manitoba
Where the wheat and maples grow.

It journeyed through Saskatchewan
On fertile, level plain,
Through foothills of Alberta
Crossing fields of golden grain.

At length it reached the grandeur
Of the Rocky Mountain peaks,
Crossed scenic British Columbia
Like double silver streaks,

Passed through dense swampy muskeg
Over slippery ice and snow
The blue Pacific Ocean
Was as far as it could go.

Attacked by savage winter months,
Delayed by granite rocks,
Thick undergrowth in forests
And severe financial blocks.

When the long hard trip had ended
Do you know what came alive?
Canadian Pacific Railway
In the year 1885.

HARVIE JOHNSTONE

HARVIE was born some time in 1929 (and even that's hearsay), and hasn't yet died. He was more or less educated at Orillia Collegiate Institute (pre-Orillia District Collegiate & Vocational Institute) and Ryerson (Graphic Arts), both of which he says he failed miserably. Harvie took the easy way out and went into a career in journalism, where he could never keep a job. Radio Station CFOR hired him as news editor. Peter McGarvey, the station manager, saw his talents as a news organizer and encouraged Harvie to join the RCAF which was beckoning pilots for the Korean war. Seeing what a threat pilots like him were, the North Koreans surrendered.

From there it was from one newspaper to another, from the *Brockville Recorder and Times* as sports editor to *The Globe and Mail* as wire editor. He kept getting promoted out of the way where he could do less harm. Having run out of publications who'd hire him, Harvie and his wife started their own little called the *Barrie Banner*. Since Harvie appointed himself publisher and editor, nobody could fire him. They sold the *Banner* to some group called the *Toronto Star* and Harvie went to the *Globe*.

Tired of commuting and terrified of traffic jams, Harvie squirreled his way onto the faculty at Georgian College, where he stuck out teaching all those things he had failed at in his working career to unsuspecting journalism and communications students.

Harvie was finally promoted by the college to the role of farmer just outside the Village of Forest Home. He thinks they called it retirement.

The Magic Harness

'Twas last Christmas Eve and in the horse stable
Only one was astir, and that was old Mabel.
She sensed something shuffling somewhere in the mow
And knew 'twas too soon for the mouser to me-e-eow.
Now Chester and Bailey were snoozing away
While Bruzer and Opie seemed stuffed full of hay.
First Stretch and then Sonny, then Bruzer and Roo,
Then Shadow and Babes blinked wide awake too.

'Twas Beekay the Barn Kat and Roquefort the Rat
Who usually stirred up the barn with their spat.
The horses were curious, the stalls were all still;
A sensation was spreading: that of goodwill.
Meanwhile in the mow, the hay was a-stirring.
The mouser called BeeKay had just begun purring.
Then suddenly out popped a jolly old elf
Could this be the one some called Santa Himself?

But how could this be? No harness a-jingle?
No reindeer and bells? No sleigh for Kris Kringle?
Well – a few lumpy bags and some string in a ball.
Oh – a little toy sleigh. But that's really all.
"My reindeer were tired from their long jaunt today,
So I hoped you could help me the rest of the way.
Donder and Blitzen and all of the boys
I sent back," Santa said, "where they make all the toys.

"They've pulled me from China o'er mountains and seas
To the chimneys in Asia and Europe with ease.
Across the Atlantic to Canada now –
But here's where my reindeer have taken their bow.
Now if you'd slip into this small ball of string,
We'll hitch up this sleigh (a wee bit of a thing)."
"But the string is so tiny," some horses said.
"It would snap into bits if we tugged on your sled."

"Not to fret," twinkled Santa, his nose all aglow.
"My magic string-harness, if you really must know,
Is a fits-all device that will expand and then shrink
To suit anyone when I give it a wink."
So the horses relented, slipped into the string;
And they felt the string strengthen, go zangety-zing.
Tho' the sleigh just got bigger, the load seemed to lighten.
And as Santa climbed on, the stars seemed to brighten.

"Next thing we should know," said Chester and Roo,
"Is: Who'll replace Rudolph to light up our crew?"
"Babes knows a harness," Santa then said.
"I know she could easily lead off our sled."
So BeeKay the BarnKat and Roquefort the Rat
Joined forces that day after patching their spat.
Together with horses – Santa in tow –
This unlikely team set our Christmas aglow.

Those Weapons of Math Instruction

A teacher was nabbed at the airport today
His tools were seized by deduction.
The Mounties declared he had quite an array --
His Weapons of Math Instruction.

His collection of ruler, protractor and square,
His slide-rule and sharp little pen
Were proof of a link to some evil affair,
So the cops locked him up in a den.

Al-Gebra, that infamous black-bearded gang,
Was surely his terrorist link.
Its members used code names like "X" and a "Y"
And the suspect sketched those with red ink.

Isosceles said, "If with me you'll bear,
Each triangle has but three sides.
Side four," he was sure, "makes sort of a square
Behind which each terrorist hides."

Al-Gebrans solve problems with all sorts of means
And refer to the cells as "unknowns."
They use, so they claim, just any extremes
With co-ordinates nobody owns.

The square root of June can never be pi
Nor even the cubed root of May.
To make sense of it all needs a bit of a lie
To foil any further foul play.

No one can be sure if he's guilty or pure –
He's guilty until proven clean.
Young victims are drawn into rooms to endure
Brain-washing that's really quite mean.

Al-Gebrans, I'm told, will a cubicle hold
As those villains go off quite tangential.
Their motives unmixed, their methods quite bold,
Their murderous plots quite potential.

So a fella named Bush told all evil-doers
To 'fess up or face real perdition.
He kept his hands clean (not one of those boors)
By a method he just called "rendition."

Now Dubya declared, that God vowed to him:
"You'll have lots more tools for deduction:
More fingers and toes to count with a whim,
To add Weapons of Math Instruction."

What's a Rainbow For?

I wonder what a rainbow's for? It can't be just for viewing.
And why do birds above me soar while I'm stuck here a-stewing?
Perhaps the rainbow's view of me is equally unfounded.
And birds no doubt are glad that I am,
like the trees, just grounded.
Now is Aurora's quivering dance
With Borealis just by chance?
Those Northern Lights: I'm quite content
To greet in awe their dazzlement.

Combing a Swamp: A Mucky Business

Richard is the only person I know who had a 200-acre farm of which 40 acres was in hay and 350 square miles was swamp. His 18 cows, intellectually superior creatures at best, preferred the swamp.

I should clarify that this swamp search occurred many years ago when Richard was just a kid and I wasn't much older. A similar tracking we did recently, combing the swamp for his missing animals reminded me of that long-ago slosh:

When you try to find cows in a swamp, do you know how loudly they bawl? They don't. They hold their breath so you don't even smell cow-breath when you pass 18 inches in front of the herd. They stare at you, snickering quietly to each other. Back then he had milk-cows, cows that looked like OPP cars -- Holsteins or something.

So when we did locate them, it wasn't because of their raucous behavior, it was because Richard tripped over one. How, you ask, do you trip over a cow? Well there's not much above swamp level to bump into when the cow's up to its udder in mudder,

It was our second major foray into the muck and we found oodles of tracks both times. First foray was from the west, second from the east.

Richard's faithful dog accompanied us on both trips, helpful as can be. He scampered, if scampering is the word when he's hip-deep in quagmire, every which way, probably bounding over bovine backs thinking they were fallen logs, tongue trailing through the mud, but reporting back: No cows. His dog was always such a big help.

Richard's farm was on the edge of west Orillia, north of the hamlet of Forest Home. His swamp, just south of the Barrie Road, drains from all directions, but probably oozes and strains very slowly into the core of the earth, causing eruptions and earthquakes in Afghanistan and Japan.

A few years later, not because of his wayward beasts, but because he was probably just tired of milking 250, or so it seemed, cows, he got out of the dairy cow business.

Now, fast-forward to more recently when his new herd of beef cattle, Scotch Shorthorns, vanished.

It was a hot blistering day, too hot for us mere humans, let alone cows, to be caught in the midday sun. Oh, we combed the swamp as we had years before, knee-deep or worse in muck. Richard opined as how maybe the swamp had expanded somewhat and was no longer a mere 350 square miles.

Time for a glass of buttermilk, we finally agreed, This was after what, I for one, was sure must have been several weeks sploshing around.

The sun was setting and the day was no longer so hot that creatures had to seek shade. "Might as well throw some hay down to the stable," Richard sighed. "We've got a cow and a new calf down there that can't go hungry tonight."

He continued: "We'll have to look for the cows again tomorrow. We'll never find them in the swamp with a flashlight if we can't find them in daylight."

Richard tossed a couple of bales down the chute from the mow. Then he went down to the stable.

"Toss down some more bales," Richard said. "All the cows are here."

And sure enough, no dummies they, the cows had known when to come in out of the hot sun. They had come in through an open door and probably spent much of the day, munching what little hay was left over from the day before. Unlike us they had spent the day in the shade. I think I heard one of them snicker.

Sound Siphon Stirred Crazy Mixed-up Leaves

Early this past fall, you were going to have packed that mountain of leaves into plastic bags to save for mulch, or -- naughty, naughty -- set out for the trash person to pick up. You didn't. How could you know about the big squall just waiting for you to finish raking?

You may feel it's unsporting that you have to rake your leaves twice this year. Although hard to believe, it's all traceable to a little gadget called a sound siphon.

Now you who are technically disoriented will by now have forgotten the Barrie-Oro-Orillia (BOO) Airport sound siphon. This device, invented a couple of years ago by a few tech professors who had a lot of time on their hands at Georgian College, would suck up all the horrid airport sounds that neighbouring farmers grumbled about. Each farmer was to receive one and fire it up during airplane takeoffs so their sheep wouldn't scare off the coyotes, or something.

To satisfy the farmers, a BOO champion had challenged the tech professors to come up with something like a vacuum cleaner, but it should suck up sound instead of dust. So they did.

"To put it simply," the tech wizards said back then, "you just flick this switch and the decibel inverter compresses the incoming sound waves. Then this No. 3a distending assimilator encircles outgoing waves and undopplers them."

They explained that it works a bit like a sponge inside a bag and, periodically, the sponge would have to be replaced to prevent the bags from bursting and unleashing all those compressed little decibels.

As a result of this, BOO officials worked out a deal with the farmers. But they forgot to mention HOW to replace the sponges and dispose of them (the sponges, not the farmers) by tying them to NASA rockets which were to be fired at the sun.

Now back to your pile of leaves. Overnight Monday this past week you may have noticed a bit of a draft in Simcoe County, a draft that seemed to be about 237 miles an hour which, converted to metric is awfully breezy. This draft donated your nicely tied-down winter pool cover in Simcoe County to a neighbor in Chicoutimi. It also moved a lot of leaves, your leaves, which you had so proudly weighted down with a strip of birch bark.

Well, that breeze was not just your average Act of God. A few airport neighbours had decided 'twas time to replace their sound suction sponges. They'd heard about a couple on the next concession road who'd hiked off to Florida to dispose of their sponges. The Georgian wizards didn't tell anybody that compressed sound energy is apt to turn into a frenzied squall. Nobody ever proved what caused Hurricane Andrew.

"Heck," the farmers decided at an Oro community meeting, "we can't afford to go to Florida. Let's just dispose of these sponges in Lake Simcoe." And so they did. As a result, your neatly piled leaves are somewhere in Quebec and you acquired more than twice as many a few feet deep on your lawn, probably from Ohio.

HEATHER GOSEIN-LESKA

HEATHER is a Communications Professor at Georgian College in Barrie, a real estate professional, a copywriter and a barbeque girl for her husband's meat and delicatessen business. Whenever she manages to find spare time, she enjoys writing poetry and short stories with no particular theme in mind. Her inspiration often derives from Lake Simcoe, on the shores of which she and her husband have their cottage/home.

Filigree

Intense, intricate
it shattered
while I watched
in fascination
unwilling to intercede

Insistent, insinuating
I languished
before shared intent
impeded inspiration

Infinite, incisive
across time
boundaries fell
I shivered
Inamorato

Of Prisms and Pathos

Pathos trumps irony when cliché becomes truth
confluence of life-poetry hidden by fiction
internal dichotomy threatens evisceration
of the everyday
laundry waits, dishes soak, obliterated
words consume accessibility of the mind
dreamless morning shattered by a ringing phone
unmade bed mocks Canadian geese
skimming frozen surface of the lake
prismatic reflection of the mundane.

Wind Storm

Elemental music infused my world
On that gray, green December day
When I longed for your touch
Across the water

Whitecaps roiled
Against rock shoreline
House shuddered
With weight of the wind

And I marked on
Hearing the incessant beat
Watching

For the moment of calm between waves
When I could reach out for you
Lost

And the day grayed into night
Without a heartbeat missed
As the house stood strong
Against the wind's attack

And I dressed for a ball.

CHRISTINE SPEAR

CHRISTINE began her writing career as a result of being a hybrid from an English Scholar mother and a dramatic, theatre-loving father. Both parents were magnificent storytellers. Her mother would send back the letters she wrote from Queen's University in Kingston with the grammar mistakes corrected. Christine has written short stories, poetry, letters and journals. She often falls asleep with a book on her chest. Lately, her focus has been the short story and creative non-fiction. Christine is a member of The Mariposa Writers' Group and the Writer's Cauldron writing group. In addition to winning the second place Short Story Contest at the Literary Lapses Festival in 2006 and again in 2009, she was a winner in the Orillia Stories Competition in *The Packet & Times* and received an Honourable Mention in Lakehead University's Writers' Workshop for poetry. Christine has also won the Association of Community Theatre President's Award for extensive work done with the Scarborough Music Theatre. Christine has had her poetry published in Sheridan College's *Portico Literary Magazine*, as well as both poetry and short fiction in the Park Street Collegiate Institute's *Yearbooks*.

Aunt Margaret: A Study in Moxie

Someone once said that Margaret Katherine Louise McGill, my mother's sister, was a party-girl. I knew the truth: she was the party. In the three pictures I see of her, the first is a black-and white from 1955 showing her standing beside a flashy Studebaker™. She is wearing a black tea dress and a two-foot-wide hat. A fur stole is draped over one arm. One hand holds a foot-long cigarette holder. Her young nieces and nephews stand nearby, open-mouthed.

The second picture, in colour, is in the 70s. Aunt Margaret poses for the camera wearing an exquisitely designed and sewn yellow sheath. She made it herself. This time the cigarette holder is shorter.

Smiling right into the camera in the last picture, Aunt Margaret shows off a hot pink, marabou-trimmed evening gown. Her fingernails painted a purple-red and matching her lipstick made eagles nervous. Grey hair and pale lips were never seen on Aunt Margaret. The cigarette holder was jeweled. *Pastel* was not in her vocabulary. Picking up her coat from cold storage one time I was startled, but not surprised, to find it was black mink with emerald green lining.

Aunt Margaret delivered on the promise her looks held. Whenever she came for a visit, she would bring treasures for us from Marshall Fields and Company. She worked there as a women's wear manager. One time she brought a dozen pairs of outrageous sunglasses. Elton John, step aside! We all got toast tongs fifteen years ahead of the Pampered Chef parties.

Then Aunt Margaret would get on the phone to set up soirées (never just parties), bridge games and theatre outings. Locals would be calling to find out when she would be arriving.

Social life for her stay was organized with the Scrabble board out and a jigsaw puzzle set up. As we grew up our Scrabble games became better, but we rarely beat her.

I never knew 'til I was into my 30s that Aunt Margaret accomplished everything on a tight budget. In the 50s, women managers were still doing poorly compared to men. The Studebaker and draped stole were borrowed. Aunt Margaret dropped out of school, but her fine sewing, daily newspaper reading and a flamboyant, unshakeable focus had her succeed as others fell by the wayside.

A cherished family story tells of the family visit to Aunt Margaret's brothers at the local "Y" camp. Everyone was to contribute something for a potluck. The boys put in the likes of Navy Bean Soup while Grandma (Margaret's mother) had baked prized butter tarts. Suddenly, Margaret grabbed the bag of butter tarts, headed for the camp rowboat and rowed out in the lake. There she devoured all twelve butter tarts. Her reckless behaviour would always say, "*Why have goulash when there are pastries to be had!*"

For Aunt Margaret's arrivals, we cleaned up our houses and our *language*. We stood up straight and pulled out our best recipes. She inspired our creativity and fear of catching the dickens for not playing full out. The night before she died, in her 70's, she had the family watching the NBA Championships.

Recently, I ran into a long lost cousin who said, "Are you ever like Aunt Margaret." Well, I'm still working on that one.

The Big Move

Taking leave of one's senses is a polite way of saying *going bonkers*. Either way, I was sure Aunt Verva Calhoun had done exactly that when I planned my twice-a-year visit to her. I was sure this visit would be different and that my ideal of a high-flying, take-no-prisoners Aunt Verva was in jeopardy. I wasn't willing to let that happen, though, so I was in an anxious sweat walking up the path to her new bungalow in the Milwaukee *burbs*.

Aunt Verva had left her chic apartment in Chicago and her lucrative job at the bridal department at Marshall Field & Company. She had taken a position with the same employer but in one of the mall stores. Now she worked in women's wear and had a bungalow instead of a chic apartment.

I'm Janet Grove, eldest niece to Miss Verva (not *Ms.* Verva which she considers an abomination as a title). As a nurse, I seem to be the one delegated to keep track of any family *deviations*.

My twice-a-year visits to see Aunt Verva used to be, my folks felt, to give me more social graces. Now that they are gone, I go because she is so much fun – graces aside. Aunt Verva always entertained me with theatre – *Les Miserables* one time. She prepared gourmet food – red snapper amandine if we were dieting and marinated pork tenderloin baked in phyllo pastry if we weren't.

I could never cultivate, to Verva's disappointment, a taste for very dry martinis. Always, I would remind her she needed James Bond in her life, to which I got *the look*. That look which said, *don't go there* consisted of eyes rolling, nostrils slightly flaring and lips pursed in scorn. I got this every time I asked Verva if she was *seeing* anyone.

With every visit, Verva would throw a soirée – never just a party.

Sometimes I think Verva did this so I would carry a message back to my small Canadian town that Verva Calhoun was leading an absolutely charmed existence.

When I arrived for the visit I thought would be different, one of her old plaques hung under her mailbox reminding her new neighborhood it was only twenty five days 'til her birthday. This drop of arrogance encouraged me – a sure sign of the old Verva.

The door opened and I was swept into a tight hug by Verva.

"You're late," she said. If Verva had said, *I'm glad to see you*, I would have been alarmed again. Ever since I can remember I was too late, too early, too thin, too something! Aunt Verva hadn't been taken over by madness after all. Dare I say peacefulness seemed to have crept into her demeanour… old agitations like drumming fingers and the rolling of the eyes in disapproval were gone. I almost suspected she was in love.

"Verva, how is all this really going?" I ventured.

"Oh," Verva replied, "quite fine – now."

"OK, Verva," I stated, "Let's hear the part between the *fine* and the *now*."

Verva smiled an acknowledgement that I had finally reached my own power around this self-made woman.

She started, "You know how I ran the women's wear fashion show in Chicago along with the bridal department?"

"Uhm," I encouraged.

"Janet, here I am to do the same. I set up a meeting with all the models. I knew they'd be different here. Oh, they were beautiful and in shape but after the show they all went home to the HHK – house, husband and kids. That is, everyone but Colleen MacGregor. The first time I saw her, my mind shrieked - *what is she doing here?*"

"She was a supermodel if I'd ever seen one. A good four inches taller than the others. She was a stunning dark brunette. She had those Scottish blue eyes you can't get with contact lenses. Anyway, I made my introductions and handed out my *Guide To A Topnotch Modeling Corps*. Goodness knows how long it took me to put that together. The models had been close to winging it while putting the shows together.

They grabbed up the guide like mad. Obviously, they were glad to have some coaching. But Colleen MacGregor casually picked up the last guide, briefly glanced at it and then threw it into her tote bag. That's the first and last time I saw her with that guide.

"Of course, I wouldn't have minded if there was any evidence she read it on her off hours. No, I caught her questioning the other models what had been in it while she polished her nails, did her exercising and arranged her clothes. I let it pass for the time being. She was such an impressive looking model. You know, she inevitably was the bride in the wedding tableau at the end of the fashion shows. We could put daisies and cornflowers in her hair for a country wedding. We could have her dripping pearls, rhinestones and feathers in high fashion. It didn't matter. She would walk out on the runway. Then there would be a gasp and wild joyful clapping. There was not one female in that audience from twelve to one hundred who didn't suddenly want to be a bride!"

"You talk about her in the past, Verva." I surmised that she'd finally taken off for the runways of New York, London and Paris.

"No, she's not with the store any longer." Verva answered with a secret smile.

Verva took a deep breath as if she was launching into the biggest part of the *Colleen Story*.

"One day I ran into her in the dressing room. She had one of the other women reciting the teamwork section of the guide with her while they put polish on her toenails. Trouble was, they were the team and she was the Queen of England. I asked the other women to step outside – that I needed to speak to Colleen. She didn't say a word – just stared at me. The thing was, she knew she was out of line – lording it over everyone. Colleen was playing small and she knew it, but Colleen wasn't going to admit it.

I said to her, Verva continued, *"You don't fit here and you know it.*

Colleen started speaking with an incredible sadness, "I can't…"

86

You can't, I cut in, you can't seem to do anything here. You don't follow anyone's rules but your own.

Colleen persisted " I can't… because… I can't read," she stammered.

Well! Janet! Colleen and I just looked at each other for a long time. Then I told Colleen she would report to my home every night after work for now," Verva said.

So, Aunt Verva Calhoun was momentarily stopped. But I knew the family story about Verva – how the school dropout had gotten endless reading lessons from her aunts – all of them teachers. The wailing and complaining they endured was legendary. Colleen had no escape now.

The next evening and for many following, Colleen reported to Verva's. There, Verva fed Colleen gourmet meals and discussed current events. But most of all she hammered the hows and whys of reading into that beautiful head and read, read, read to her.

Now Milwaukee is not really on the flight path between Los Angeles, New York and Europe, but about three months ago, if you were looking, you might have seen a stunning woman in a stylish car drive out from the Milwaukee airport to a small bungalow in the Milwaukee burbs. She slipped into the house where an attractive older woman waited. Together they prepared haute cuisine, discussed presidents' and prime ministers' policies and read, read, read… to each other.

Kingsley's Piano

I have always felt people who had visions were slightly suspect – 'til I had one. It happened in the summer and I was just waking up. A black man was standing in my room. He said quietly, "I am here now." Then he was gone. I wasn't doing drugs, my eyes were wide open and craziness wasn't in style then – so he had to be a "vision."

Shortly after that I was in a seminar that encouraged us to "live outside of the dots" of our lives. There I met John White, a black musician and music promoter who was always on the lookout to introduce people to his bands.

Captivated by music all my life, I was enthralled to get close to the people who played it. It was the 1980s and one of the happiest times I can remember. We were fearless – especially women. In Toronto, if you couldn't sleep, you could jump into your car and go downtown for some of the finest live music this side of New York.

The destination was not the usual clubs though. These were the days when "last call" in Ontario was at 12:15 am. Trouble was, the musicians weren't ready to quit and neither were their audiences.

This gave rise to "after hours" spots. In these places, it was okay to play 'til dawn. After their regular gigs, musicians packed up their instruments and headed to a spot I frequented – Muhtadi's. It was nothing to have four horns, five saxophones, keyboards and drums jamming all night.

Muhtadi, a Trinidadian, played the big bongos and won awards for his cooking. He had rented a warehouse room, stuck a stage in the corner and set up cabaret style. We listened 'til our hearts were full of calypso, rock, jazz and the blues. We ate 'til our bellies were full of the Caribbean. Every time I left Muhtadi's this song from "Guys and Dolls" ran through my brain: "When the smell of the rain washed pavement comes up clean and fresh and cold; and the streetlights glare fills the gutters with gold; that's my time of day, my time of day…"

At Muhtadi's I first encountered a soon-to-be world class keyboard man – Kingsley Ettienne. After most of the after hours crowd had gone home, I noticed a man across the room having an impassioned conversation at another man. I say "at" as "with" just wouldn't be true. My promoter friend, John White, a whole other story himself, had fallen asleep on a divan. I was happily listening to the music and observing this fascinating conversation, though too far away to hear it.

Once I got to know Kingsley, I would know this conversation inside out. It was about what a hard time black musicians had in this town. Was it true? Maybe. I'll never know. What I knew was that every time I went out to hear these bands, it was a gift. It was like going to a foreign country without the expense.

At some stage, I was introduced by John to Kingsley of the passionate conversation. After that he sometimes visited my home and my piano was played and played. Always, his parting comment was, "Chris, I need that piano." And every time I protested with, "I grew up with a piano; it's part of my heritage."

This piano was a beautiful mahogany upright – Mason & Risch – a castoff from The Royal Conservatory of Music when The Conservatory put in new Yamahas. With my parents doing local musicals, the piano of my youth had given so many memories.

"Chris, I need your piano" went on for a good year – a game we played a lot. Along with that game, I learned first hand the struggles musicians had. There were the competitions for gigs, expensive studio time to record and even more expensive lessons needed to surpass their own skills and keep up.

Then one day, I found myself in a hospital losing a baby I had tried twenty years to get. Heartsick though I was, I understood acutely what my dream was. Someday I'd be getting my child. I knew that for sure.

What I also got at that time, was that I was a stepping stone, hiding under water – maybe the stone that was keeping someone else from realizing his dream.

Out of hospital, the next day, I started arrangements to get one seldom-used piano to a new owner – Kingsley. Sure, I had played it, both hands too – just not at the same time.

Kingsley said very little when I told him it was coming. I think he was as shocked as I was that it was really happening. Smiling, I sent that piano out the door with the movers and a "Baby, are you ever going to get a workout!"

Kingsley couldn't even be home to take delivery – "Have to be in the studio." His lady-love, Betty Richardson, a fine performer herself, took delivery. I held my breath as the movers almost dropped the piano struggling to lift it over the small porch. My dread and I disappeared after it finally passed the front door.

A week or so later I went to "visit" the piano. Momentarily, I was stunned. Its rich brown had been painted shiny ebony! At next glance, I saw it had been painted beautifully, like a work of art. It was being kept in a small, freshly-painted room under lock and key. Two pictures of jazz greats hung on the wall. This piano was being cherished as it had never been cherished before. But at no time was it cared for more than the hours and hours Kingsley spent playing it, "getting his chops down."

Now it was my time to have the upper hand in our piano game. I teased him with every milestone he passed on his climb to international status – a university music degree, his own compositions, CDs with him at the keyboard *and* doing vocals and on and on. I would tell him that it had nothing to do with him; it was really because of my old piano.

Somehow along the way we've lost touch. That baby dream is now my fine, real-live son who turned sixteen a few weeks ago.

But, I remember those days like they were yesterday. We never even entertained the idea of an unsafe world. It was a time we loved recklessly and passionately. It was a time we were bigger than ourselves. It was the time of Kingsley's piano.

JIM BUTLER

JIM was born in Montreal and is married to Elspeth Jewett. They have one daughter, Susan Elspeth. He graduated Concordia (B.Sc.) and has several subsequent years in the Commerce Faculty. He was admitted to the American Society of Real Estate Counselors in 1987. Jim Joined Marathon Realty Company in February, 1974 and was moved to Toronto in a corporate relocation transfer in 1981. Following a career in Property Management operations, Jim developed a separate functional national group specializing in Asset and Buildings Technology. He retired in 1993 settled with his wife in Bayshore Village. The Butlers developed an interest in dogs, specifically Doberman Pinschers. They were active in canine conformation and obedience shows. Jim has also been interested in digital photography for the last seven to eight years.

Jim has served in various capacities at the Real Estate Institute of Canada, Institute of Real Estate Management (Chicago), Montreal Building Owners and Managers Association (BOMA), Rotary Clubs of Montreal and Lagoon City, Orillia and the District Canadian Club. Jim is a Charter member of the Orillia Probus Club.

Jim's writing includes: monthly articles (with photos) for *The Packet & Times* reporting speakers at monthly meetings of the Orillia and District Canadian Club; *Property Management Procedures Manual, Tech Tips,* various trade related and technical papers prepared for a variety of professional organizations. Jim has also been a speaker at various business, building and real estate conferences in Canada.

Technology Futures

My father-in-law died in 1938, 16 years before our marriage. My dad died in 1942. Consequently, we were both unable to meet these major players in the early lives of our spouses. Probably, due to this circumstance, we have from time to time speculated about the likely result if we were able to introduce our dads to current technology and living conditions.

Imagine the absolute fright that they would experience if they were to find themselves in the middle lane of highway 401 at any time of the day, based on their respective experiences with then-current two-lane road systems. The comparison is the family minivan of today with a 1940 Chevy or Ford – although my father-in-law did not own an automobile and traveled around the city on streetcars.

In 1940 homes, central heating meant coal-fired furnaces producing hot water that circulated through cast iron piping to room radiators and shoveling the ashes from the firebox as well as putting them out for collection twice weekly. Today, electric, natural gas or heating-oil fired systems linked to forced air circulation ducting and automatic thermostatic controls would seem amazingly reliable and convenient by contrast. Frost-free refrigerators with ice-cube makers and the convenience of home freezers would seem a wonderful substitute for the root cellars and the 'ice-boxes' which were dependent on daily delivery of 35 or 50-pound blocks of ice to preserve our food.

Central air-conditioning systems sharing the automatic thermostats and ventilation ductwork used by the heating system to preserve in-house comfort would seem magical to someone who relied on electric fans, a seat on the front porch hoping for a breeze, a trip to the lake or an ice cream cone to offset the heat of summer.

Domestic housekeeping has been greatly simplified by the development of automatic washers and driers to replace wringer washers and the backyard clothesline. Automatic dishwashers now simplify and sanitize the work previously performed by the greasy tepid dishpan in the kitchen sink, followed by the manually applied dishtowel. Replacement of the Bissel carpet sweeper by high efficiency vacuum cleaners and the 'treadle' Singer™ sewing machines by the current automatic marvels have contributed a great deal to easier and faster work around the house. Electric ranges and ovens, automatic can openers and the ever-ready microwave have all added to simplification of the homemaker's art.

The functionality of digital photography would be unbelievable to folks who had been reliant on the Kodak Brownie. In-home ink-jet printing of photographs would add to the wonder. I would greatly enjoy introducing my dad to the computer and word processing as a substitute to the old Remington manual typewriter. Ballpoint pens compare favorably with fountain pens and inkwells. Electronic voice recorders in the business world replaced dictation of correspondence to a shorthand stenographer or to the wax cylinder machine which was slow, distorted and manually erased after each use.

Colour television transmitted by 300 channels, including newscast reports of events around the world, would be a far cry from radio stations and daily newspapers as the source of information and entertainment. Universal Internet access and e-mail now simplifies research for scholastic or business world purposes and replaces Canada Post and thousand volume phonebook collections. In-home DVD movie collections now enhance leisure-time amusement previously accomplished by bundling up on a cold winter night to trudge over to the local cinema.

My wife remembers her father's dislike of 'canned music'; he believed the only way to listen to music would be an evening at the symphony. Modern hi-fi stereo equipment and the clarity of CDs would change his thinking about this experience as well; the convenience and the quality of sound reproduction using modern equipment would cause our ancestors to marvel.

But these domestic advances are minor in comparison to the wonder of developments in medical technology, techniques and pharmaceuticals that have greatly increased the normal life span of modern man. Indeed, both fathers would possibly still have been with us if modern medical capabilities could have been accessed. But this is a subject for a separate discussion.

The Wright brothers made the first controlled, powered and sustained heavier-than-air human flight on December 17, 1903. Comparison of their aircraft and the propeller-driven British Spitfire or the early Cessna or Piper Cub monoplanes used during the Second World War with more recent airliners and jet fighters normal to current aviation would amaze earlier generations. And, of course, the last forty years have seen the addition of the beginnings of space travel to human accomplishments.

I have visited the computer museum in Boston, which features 'Eniac', the computer used to develop the atom bomb. Racks of angle-iron braces fill a room larger than the living room of a large house. The braces support perforated metal sheet shelving holding some 18,000 vacuum tubes. The system routinely functioned for seconds before a tube burned out, which required an attendant to search through the stacks to find where the replacement was needed.

The Wikipedia Encyclopedia website entry reports:

"Until the mid-1970s, most computer access was via punched cards. Programmes and data…were punched by hand on a keypunch machine and read into a card reader. Large computing sites such as Columbia University purchased cards by the truckload and furnished them free of charge to users. During the IBM 360 era (1969-80) Columbia's cards were embossed with the legend "CUCC 360" (Columbia University Computer Center IBM 360) and the Columbia shield (*In Lumine Tuo Videbimus Lumen*).

The pink "job card" (the first card in a deck) was preprinted with the essentials of JCL job-card syntax. Cards were available in assorted colors, allowing colour-coding of different sections of a deck such as JCL, programme source, data.

Operators of "Key-Punch machines" spent their working days punching the holes to feed characters into the computers. The Eniac computer (initially developed in 1939 by the U.S. Army to calculate ballistic firing patterns) boasted less computing power than the hand held Canadian 'Blackberry' unit or even, if the truth be told, less power than the common hand held calculators used by high school students. Each programming card is now replaced by pressing a single button on the keyboard of such calculators.

Environmental control in modern office towers with sealed glass windows is accomplished by completely automated centralized systems capable of monitoring and adjusting temperature and ventilation at individual desk positions through electronic control mechanisms on each of the variable air volume damper actuators throughout the building. Each of these units can monitor air temperature and blend heated and super-chilled air to satisfy comfort demands based on system programming. These systems also control building lighting and allow the building operator to modify the 'lights on' and 'lights off' system commands as they apply to individual work positions. Building security systems control after-hours access and monitor of each door and elevator in the complex electronically, supported, where needed, by closed circuit television equipment.

Science Fiction writers have anticipated most technology innovations. Isaac Asimov developed the concept of Robotics and created the three laws planned to govern robot intelligence. Ben Franklin's work is known. Leonardo da Vinci in the fifteenth century left sketches of the helicopter, submarine and a host of other then unknown but since invented fundamentals of modern life.

The history of technological development through the centuries demonstrates exponential growth in our rate of change such as comparison of the first Wright Brothers monoplane in 1903 to the current NASA space programme. Perhaps the universe reflected by the Star Trek series will become a part of everyday life in the not-too-distant future.

Barn Swallows

It was Spring and the pair of Barn Swallows, resplendent in their purple upper body feathers and rusty breasts, returned to the peninsula jutting out from the east shore of Lake Simcoe. With unerring precision, they located the building (not a barn in this case, but the front door of a human residence) that had sheltered their family for generations. The nest above the front door had been removed by the winds during the previous autumn, so they started on the immediate priority of rebuilding on an impossibly narrow ledge above the front door.

The Swallow family of birds, as described in the National Geographic *Field Guide to Birds of North America* (1983), has "slender bodies with long, pointed wings resembling Swifts, but the wrist angle is sharper and farther from the body and flight is more fluid. Adept aerialists, Swallows dart to catch flying insects. Flocks perch in long rows on rooftops and wires."

The nest is securely anchored to a ledge only an inch in depth, about eight inches below the eaves of the house. It is formed with twigs and bits of straw reinforcing an adobe-like mud shape some six to seven inches long by about four inches wide; the base tapers down to the wall of the house. The design is structurally reliable. The construction material for the nest is carried, bit-by-bit, from mud puddles and fields (or in this case lawns) to the construction site. The interior surface of the nest is lined by the mother bird with soft white feathers in preparation for the miracle of birth, which is to follow.

Another potential family had settled on the opposite side of the house, having reclaimed an equally precarious perch, under the eaves, below the roof. Swallows rely on a mutual support system; during periods of important family events needs or danger, reinforcements are called in to assist the couple in their celebrations or in home defence.

The Swallows had returned to a familiar spot; they paid little attention to the residents of the house, apparently aware that they had nothing to fear from these humans. The relationship is mutually beneficial; the birds gain a sheltered spot to build the nest. The humans tolerate the streaks of guano on the house siding and the mailbox (although the parents do try to help with the cleanup; they are often observed stopping to pick up a lump of waste and carry it away when outward bound searching food. This is probably an innate instinct to disguise the location of the nest). The humans are provided with weeks of interest and amusement as the annual mystery unfolds. The humans appreciate the impact by the Swallows on the cloud of midges which forms over the driveway each year in May and June; the Swallows found the source of food to be another benefit.

In previous years, the nesting pair had produced and raised three juveniles. This year, five eggs were formed and hatched; dad, with some assistance from mom and further support from the extended family on the other side of the house, worked frantically to fill gaping maws; the rapid development of the babies demanded frequent feeding. The parents recuperated briefly as babies rested between meals.

The family quickly began to outgrow the nest, which nature had designed to accommodate two adults and three infants. As the babies grew, conditions became quite crowded. Finally, the largest of the babies had developed the wing and tail feathers needed to support flight; one morning he pushed a little too far over the edge in his efforts to be first to reach the incoming food. Falling, the wings spread instinctively and the tiny body fluttered to the support of a coach lamp over the garage door. The baby clinging desperately to it's perch, mom and dad swooped to the rescue, closely followed by the neighbours in an explosion of excited chirping and commenced the process of convincing the juvenile to accept and celebrate freedom. By mid afternoon, baby had gained the confidence needed to control flight and begin the new generation.

JOAN (MARVEN) DAULBY

JOAN moved to Ontario from Vancouver in 1965 where she met her husband, Frank in the quaint little town of Whitby, married and has lived in Ontario ever since. When Joan retired from her career in Real Estate Management, she was given the opportunity to revisit her joy of writing. To date, Joan has completed a number of short stories and poems and is working on her book, Hermit's Bluff, which is nearing completion.

In November 2006, Joan was searching for someone with whom to share her enthusiasm for writing and joined the Mariposa Writers Group.

In August 2007 Joan entered Lake Country Literary Lapses Event and won third prize in the Short Fiction Story category for her story, *Moments Shared*, and also won third prize in the Poetry Category for her poem, *To Kiss and Hug You Back*.

Joan has read her short stories at many events and, since branching out into Children's Stories, she has also read to school children and at the Ontario March of Dimes Conference in June 2009.

Joan wishes to share her third prize entries with you as well as a chapter from her book, *Hermit's Bluff*.

Moments Shared

Sophie was sitting at the kitchen table with her fingers spread wide like a fan, an assortment of nail polish and small boxes spread out before her when she heard footsteps coming across the porch.

"Hello," Gramma called out as she peered through the screen door. "Anyone home?"

"I'm in the kitchen, Gramma," Sophie hollered. "Are you staying for dinner?"

"Why, yes I am," Gramma said as she let herself in; the screen door acknowledging her entry with a familiar whapping sound as it slammed shut behind her.

"Mom had to slip out to the store….something about no cheese for her sauce….she should be back any minute," Sophie mumbled as Gramma sat down beside her.

"What are you doing to your fingers?"

"Painting them. Actually," Sophie giggled, "I'm not painting my fingers, I'm painting my nails. I have a date for the school dance tonight--a big date and he's getting his dad's car!"

"So, you'll be riding in style!" Gramma replied as she examined the arrangement of goodies. "What's in all those little boxes?"

"Oh, those are the sparkles I'm putting on my nails. You see, I choose a colour and paint one nail. Before it dries, I carefully choose one of the sparkles--a star, a moon, or a triangle and place it on the wet polish to make a design."

"Oh, my!" exclaimed Gramma as she grabbed her glasses from the chain around her neck and placed them on her nose. "I can barely see those little sparkles--even with my reading glasses. How in the world are you going to place those little bitty things on your nails, let alone make a design?"

"Watch, I'm about to start!" Sophie chose a colour and painted her left thumb nail. Then she took a wooden stick that was sharpened to a pencil point, licked it, touched one of the sparkles and carefully placed it onto her wet nail. She quickly licked her stick two more times and transported two more sparkles to her thumb to complete her design.

Gramma sat silently watching, holding her breath each time Sophie carried a sparkle to its new home on her nail. Once all the sparkles were in place and the nail was dry, Sophie took the clear polish and painted overtop of them. "See, Gramma," Sophie said as she proudly displayed her new nail, blowing on it to enhance the drying process. "Once the clear polish is dry, the sparkles will be cemented in place and will be able to dance along with me all night."

"My, my," Gramma commented thoughtfully. "We never had such things when I was a girl. And you going to the dance in a car!" she repeated, staring off as though she were looking through a window into the past. "I remember when I was your age, your Grampa would come to pick me up with his dad's horse and buggy. I used to sit on the porch swing and watch him coming up the road," Gramma sighed and turned to Sophie. "But that was a long time ago. Now, tell me about your new beau?"

"Well, he's in my science class. He has dark wavy hair and the bluest eyes you've ever seen. AND, most important of all, he is taller than I am!" Sophie confirmed with the nod of her head and a wide grin. Gramma always marveled at her height. This past year, she had grown so quickly she now stood taller than anyone in her class--including the boys! She noted that Sophie's bright blue eyes sparkled whenever she smiled and her length of curly blonde hair bounced whenever she moved.

"Gram, tell me about the dances you and Grampa used to go to."

"Well, we never had a school gymnasium for dancing and if we wanted exercise, we went outside."

"Where would you have your dances then?"

"Oh, we had dance halls! Grand dance halls that were spread out around the countryside. As I was saying, Grampa would arrive to pick me up with his dad's horse and buggy. The coat on his horse would be glistening in the sunshine and the buggy would be so clean there wasn't a speck of dirt or dust on it." Sophie didn't notice, but she had stopped painting her nails and was sitting, listening and looking in awe at her Gramma.

"Then...," Sophie prompted. "Go on..."

"Being the gentleman that he was, your Grampa would come around and help me up into the buggy. He always had his mom's favourite quilt on the back of the seat in case it got cold later. The dance hall was quite a ways down the road and it would take us most of the afternoon to get there. As we travelled, we would meet our friends who would be driving their own buggies and we would form quite a procession going along the road, one after the other. We used to laugh and joke about being a wagon train heading west to settle in the mountains and build our own town." Gramma chuckled at the memory.

"Seeing as most of us came from so far away, there would be a banquet laid out for us when we arrived--all included in the price of our ticket. There was a large covered area with a firepit in the centre and lots of tables and we'd all crowd in together. We would be famished by the time we got there and would eat like there was no tomorrow. When we finished eating, we would sit facing the fire, singing songs until we heard the band warming up."

"Did they have a stage for the band?" What was the dance hall like, Gramma? Was it very big?

"I recall everything as being big. The hall was an old log building that must have been built in my great grandparents day. It had moss stuffed between the logs to keep out the drafts and an old pot belly stove in one corner. It was really just a huge open room with chairs around the outside wall and a small stage up front for the band. Sometimes there would be eight or nine members playing instruments. There were trombones, trumpets, drums, a couple of violins and an old piano. Of course, there were singers as well. The music was wonderful! We'd all be dressed in our Sunday best and would dance until our legs could hardly support us anymore.

"I remember we girls had a contest once to see who could swish their skirts the most. We laughed and laughed as we tried harder and harder to be the best 'swisher' that ever was!" Sophie watched, fascinated as Gramma told her story. "Oh, those were the times, Sophie.

Those were the times...," Gramma reminisced.

"Gram, how did you get home? It would be very late when the dance was over and you had a long trip. Wouldn't your parents be worried?"

"In those days, there was a house--like a Bed and Breakfast--situated about halfway between the dance hall and our homes. It was appropriately known as the 'Halfway House' --Williams' Halfway House. That was the name of the owners--Williams. Fancy remembering their name after all these years.

"The house stood only feet from the roadway, straight and tall with rows of windows on the upper floor. Anyway, there were about ten rooms on the second floor, each with a single bed. The rooms were so tiny there was barely enough space for a bedside table.

"We would all arrive at the 'halfway house' with our buggies. The boys would unhitch the horses and stable them while the girls would go inside and pick the best rooms. Of course, I now realize the rooms were all alike, but we didn't think so then.

"The people who owned the home, the Williams, kept track of the dances and were always up, waiting our arrival. They went to the same church as we did and got to know our parents fairly well. Otherwise, I am not sure that we would have been allowed to travel so far to a dance and stay overnight. I used to think Mr. Williams sat at the end of the hall all night to make sure we stayed put."

"Awesome! You mean you all slept at this house? All of you?"

"We sure did! We used to look forward to it. Mrs. Williams would make us the best breakfast we had ever had the pleasure of eating pancakes, waffles, eggs, bacon, ham. Anything you wanted. They made sure they sent us on our way in the morning with full tummies."

"Wow! Do you have any more stories?" Sophie asked.

Gramma didn't have time to answer as Sophie's mom entered the kitchen, carrying an armload of groceries. "Hi, Mom, Gramma and I have been talking. Did you know Gramma and Grampa used to go to dances by horse and buggy and would stay at a 'Halfway House?"

Sophie's mom raised her eyebrow and turned to look at the two of them--Sophie with her nails half painted and Gramma with a smile on her face.

"No, Sophie, I can't say that I have heard Gramma tell that story. I will have to get her to share it with me tonight after dinner.

Sophie and her Gramma looked at each other and smiled, a sense of something special passing between them. From then on, Sophie saw her Gramma differently, always envisioning her as a young girl, dancing and 'swishing' her skirt, and thanks to Sophie and her ability to glamorize nails, Gramma could now add nail decorating to her repertoire of knowledge.

To Kiss And Hug You Back

Years ago when I was young
My sister said to me,
You know when you grow-up some day
You won't be climbing trees!

The boys you see out playing
Who you shun so gracefully,
Will soon become your favourite sport
Not picnics, forts or trees!

One day when you go out to play
You'll see him standing tall,
And as he comes a sauntering by
Your heart will take a fall.

The thumping and a twitching
That you feel within your chest,
Is just the start of many things
You'll find that you love best.

The years will quickly pass you by,
You'll grow just like your tree.
You'll find you want those boys nearby
Not mom nor dad nor me.

In time you'll want those scraggly boys
To kiss and hug you back,
So listen to my words young one
Stand off from your attack.

My sister's eyes were full of glee
And mine were wide with fright,
To have a boy so close to me
Was not my best delight!

With hands on hips, I turned my back
And climbed my climbing tree,
My sister did not know so much
There'll be no boys for me!

Hermit's Bluff
Excerpt from this Novel

Gerry Sawyer and I drove in silence as we left the bluff area—both deep in our own thoughts of today's events. I was worried about how Vera and Zebie were making out and also wondered how Ray Arbuckle had made out at the hospital with his daughter.

"Gerry, I wonder how the children and their parents are? It has been a long day for all of them. The 'not' knowing is the worst."

"Yeah, I was thinking about the kids as well. The parents will be worried for sure."

We continued our drive to Mitchell's in silence with Gerry's hand resting on the blue boot that was lying on the front seat between us. This was not going to be easy. Just looking at the boot lying next to me, made me shiver. I knew the little girl was still out there and I did not suspect she was lost. Someone must have taken her. Why else would her boot just be lying there? Also, why no trace of her? There were a lot of questions, unanswered questions.

"Gerry, I hate this part. The Mitchells are going to be hoping that we found their little girl and all we have is a blue boot—her blue boot, probably. Here we are," Shirley Ricker said to her partner.

Gerry picked up the plastic bag with the boot and we got out of the car. This time neither of us was running. We didn't even seem to notice the wind or the snow. It felt like everything was in slow motion again. I rang the doorbell. We waited. It seemed to take forever. Then, just before I went to push the doorbell once more, the door opened.

"Hello, Mr. Mitchell," I said. "May we come in?" Gerry was standing just back of me keeping the boot from Mr. Mitchell's view.

"Hello, Detective Ricker, Detective Sawyer. Sorry I took so long to come to the door. I finally convinced Jenny to lie down on the couch. We were in the den at the back of the house. Have you any news for us?"

"Some news, yes." I looked at Gerry. I could hear Mrs. Mitchell, Jenny, coming our way.

"Detective Ricker, is that you?"

"Yes, Jenny." I waited until she approached. Ryan reached out his arm to draw her into him, protecting her from what we might have to tell them. Her eyes were red and her face was puffy. As I looked at the two of them in each other's grasp, their feelings of despair and helplessness filled the air. My heart ached for them both. How to begin...... "I'm sorry, Jenny and Ryan, we have not found Mary yet. Perhaps we could sit down while we bring you up-to-date on our search."

Ryan and Jenny led us to the den at the back of the house where they had been sitting when the doorbell rang. The noise from the storm was subdued back there—only a couple of windows up high on either side of the fireplace. The familiar scent of a wood fire greeted us as we entered the room. The flames darting in and around the wood gave a cozy, relaxing atmosphere to the den; such a sharp contrast to the weather outside and what the Mitchells were really experiencing. I could not imagine the anguish of not knowing where your child could be.

"May I take your coats?" Ryan asked bringing my thoughts back to the present.

"Thank you." Gerry and I removed our coats and handed them to Ryan. Gerry had put the bag down by the couch. We both took a seat on the couch across from Jenny. Ryan returned and sat next to her.

"Jenny and Ryan," I started, "our Canine Team found a boot. We would like you to take a look at it and tell us if you think it belongs to Mary. It is in a clear plastic bag and must stay in the bag until forensics gets a chance to check it out."

Gerry carefully reached for the bag containing the boot.

Jenny moaned and covered her mouth. Ryan grasped the bagged boot, almost caressing it as he took it upon his lap.

"Yes," Ryan said. "This is Mary's boot." He handed the boot to Jenny who was now crying out load. Jenny hugged the boot while nodding her head in confirmation.

"Mr. and Mr. Mitchell," Gerry started, "I mean Jenny and Ryan, we would like to tell you what we have done so far in our efforts to find Mary. Also, we would like to let you know how we are going to proceed later this evening and tomorrow. Are you able to carry on?"

"Yes," Ryan answered for both of them. "It would be helpful if you would tell us anything you can. Detective Sawyer, I'm afraid we are in a bit of a daze, would you mind jotting down some notes while you explain things to us? We would like to have something to refer to later this evening. At the moment, nothing seems real. I'm sure we will not be able to remember much of what you are about to tell us."

"Ryan, I don't mind at all. Shirley, why don't you explain and I'll make notes as you go along."

Jenny and Ryan turned to me and I began telling them step-by-step how we found the boot and our plans for tomorrow—continued searching by canine, getting the Emergency Response Team out, and the fact the helicopter was ready but was waiting for the storm to subside. Jenny was frantic that the Emergency Response Team was not yet out and I explained why the dog and handler had to search the area first. I told them about our neighbourhood canvassing and the trip Detective Sawyer and I planned to make to the school tomorrow.

Gerry wrote down as much as he could in point form for the Mitchells to review later. "Do you have any questions?" Gerry asked.

The Mitchells were quiet and slowly shook their heads back and forth. They had no questions. Complete misery showing in their expressions.

Gerry handed Ryan his notes. "If you think of anything at any time, please call the dispatch number on my card and they will have either Detective Ricker or me return your call. Anytime!"

Gerry and I got up to leave, searching for our coats.

"Oh, I'm sorry." Ryan said as he headed to the other room to fetch them. When he returned, he stopped in the doorway. He was clutching our coats as though they were his last hope, his last link to Mary. Gerry and I stood in silence.

"Oh yes," he mumbled as he reached out with our coats.

We all turned to Jenny who was still hugging the boot. "Jenny," I said breaking the silence. "We will need the boot for evidence. I know it is something of Mary's."

Ryan spoke up. "Darling, we are going to have to give the boot back to the detectives. Could you give it to me? Please Jenny? We have to."

Jenny slowly released her grip from the boot allowing Ryan to take it.

Ryan handed Gerry the boot and we headed towards the door. Jenny had not moved from the couch and was still crying. The notes were a good idea, as she will probably not remember much of our visit. There was nothing left to say so we shook Ryan's hand and headed out to our car.

MIKE TULP

MIKE came to Canada in 1957. He obtained a Master's Degree in Social Work and enjoyed a career in Ontario Government Services After living in various communities in Ontario, he settled in Orillia in 1974 with his wife and two children.

During the past few years, Mike has been working on writing his autobiography, called *Footprints in History are not Made Sitting Down*. He hopes to summarize this in memoir form and wants to have it published or self-published at some time in the near future. Who knows? All this keeps him busy in his retirement years.

Mike's article, "What Words Cannot Say," which tells of some his experiences while vacationing in Portugal, was published in the November 2004 issue of *Canadian Living*. Mike doesn't consider himself a writer, but he enjoys writing. Because he is hard of hearing, writing provides him with an outlet that does not require a response to what he is saying. For a limited circulation periodical called *Breaking Barriers*, Mike wrote "The Wounded Spirit" in Spring 2002; "The Right Tools" in Fall 2005; and "Silence Can be Broken" in Winter 2006.

Grandpa's Message

It's wonderful to have a loving grandpa. That's what I thought and still think. I had good parents, but they were, well, how shall I say, they were just there. My mother's father was different. I want to say a few things about him because of how he influenced me.

Living all the way in Friesland, some 200 kms. North of where my family lived in the central part of The Netherlands, we saw our grandparents only a few times each year: at Christmas time, some birthdays and, of course, during the summer when we kids were invited to spend time at their farmstead.

Now that I am a grandpa, I cannot help but think of my Frisian grandpa. Thinking of him, I honestly think we have something in common. He had people working for him on his farm in Anjum; I employed social workers in the Muskoka Centre in Gravenhurst. We both were thinkers and we were initiators. He contributed his share as a member of the Provincial Legislature, and I, less politically oriented than he was, rolled up my sleeves and developed much needed social services in the various places my family and I settled in Ontario.

Though I am not a farmer and never have been, I have inherited some characteristics from him and share his vision. That's what I find most intriguing part. We thought alike. I do things today, in this country of Canada, that he would have done and, in some ways, did in his days in his country.

Thinking back to the days when he and I stumped our way across the land he owned, me, at times, being sucked down by the heavy clay soil, holding on to his hand, I feel a shiver of excitement. I realize that this humble man, without saying much, passed on something that I could never learn from books, try as I might.

I treasure a light brown-colored, people-posing post card size picture taken long ago. The sepia picture used to stand on the mantle piece at home and my older brother sent it to me when he settled my parents' estate.

Paake, my grandpa, that is, in this picture wears a mustache. He was a slightly built man of medium height; he sits in a high-backed chair; a just visible white cuff encircles his slender wrist. In the early days, people invariably assumed a non-smiling pose, and in this picture also grandpa poses like a stern-looking country man. I guess that's how the gentleman wanted to be seen. I loved my grandpa. I was named after him. When I became a man I wanted to look like him. When my time came, I started growing a mustache, too.

The bespectacled little boy in shorts, standing forlornly between his grandparents, somewhat anxiously leaning toward his dear sister as if wanting to hide behind her, is me. My pudgy little fingers can be seen straying toward grandma's arm, seeking comfort and assurance. *"Every personal photo has emotional equity, the ability to trigger memory and unleash a variety of emotions."*[1]

"You carry a message," he once told me out of the blue when I was ten years old and the two of us were walking from the farm toward the place where his favorite horse was being fitted with a set of new, hotly shining shoes. I've never forgotten the delicious burnt smell of the place. I've often wondered what he meant to tell me that day. He never did. He died soon after.

Would you believe that I've been on a quest ever since to find out what he meant by saying these mysterious words to me? In a way, his words and his example propelled me into doing things I never thought I would be doing.

I do not know what he actually did when away from the farm, but one thing I know is that he was faithful. And so am I. Years ago, a United Church minister persuaded me to volunteer and take on a leadership role in Telecare-Lifeline, Sudbury, where we lived at the time, and Telecare-Lifeline, Canada. I followed this through and today I am in the proud possession of a 20-year pin. Orillia's telephone crisis line got started in1979. My wife and I still attend special meetings when volunteers come together for a BBQ. We had a hand in getting it off the ground; our presence counts. We show support and encouragement. It's important to us. It's important to the volunteers.

My grandpa also served for many years on boards and committees. His presence had a stimulating influence on others. He and also my father paid from their own pockets for the Christian School education of their children and I benefitted from this. He believed in his ideals. He and also my father made sure that the trees they planted would bear fruit in the next generation and the next.

This was an unbelievably rich gift he and the people of his generation bestowed on us. By the time I went to school, public and alternate schools had achieved equal status. Hearing the stories of how people wanted fairness and how they fought to gain recognition and have justice done, I came to appreciate their efforts. Their belief produced action and ultimate results. My grandfather's belief became my motivation.

The same year Telecare Orillia started, the Orillia Christian Elementary School, co-ed, independent, parent initiated, non-denominational, took its place among the other schools in this community and was another private initiative benefitting our community.

I took pride in both accomplishments, knowing that by achieving this I and the others involved added quality to the multicultural character of our city and nation. I've lived in my chosen country for more than 50 years. Like one of the pieces my wife ever so skillfully quilts into the fabric she's working on, she and I blend into the country, contributing our share.

Grandpa was not an imposing man; far from it. He just was, and so am I. Our quiet conviction adds body to what we stand for.

Paake, you're here no longer, but I want to address you, Grandpa. You suffered a period of humiliation when your father's farm was sold from under his feet, but you did not let this put you down. I've suffered a period of humiliation, too, and this time of quiet suffering forced on me a desire to question what my motives for living actually were. Things I once took pride in, I no longer did so. They were not essential. I came to see that there's more to life.

Then one day your question popped up out of a bleak nowhere. The question/statement you made wanted an answer, an affirmation. The message became clear when I was 73 years old. Believe it or not, it happened when I saw myself and my wife sitting in our dining room, providing hospitality to a recently-separated mother with two little children, five and seven years old.

We were eating spaghetti. 'Spegeti' the little boy called it. He and his little sister liked it. Every now and then we would invite them to come over and we always ate 'spegeti.'

While eating and chatting, it dawned on me what life is all about. My wife and I loved these kids like we love our grandchildren. The little boy had the same name as my wife's grandfather. A coincidence? Of course, but meaningful all the same.

The memory came to me of you, Grandpa, stroking my hair because you liked me and I was named after you. I softly stroked the boy's hair. When looking into the eyes of this father, a deprived boy, I experienced one of those singular moments when time seems to stand still. I think you know what I mean.

I wish we had taken a picture of me having the two little ones sitting on my lap, one on my left knee and the other on my right and me reading them a few stories at the end of our meal. I could feel their bodies relax as they leaned into me. It deeply touched me.

We love kids, and we love them even more when they respond to our love. You had it right Paake. You showed this message of love. Because you loved me, as others did, I should add, I learned to love without reserve. We take people into our hearts and homes not because of status or name; we do so because we love them. Isn't this what you meant when you said, "You carry a message?" You carried this message to me because you lived the message.

Let's shake hands, strong hands, grandpa to grandpa. That's what I want to tell you in farewell.

1 Michael Deblich, *The Globe and Mail*, February 19, 2001.

ELIZABETH (LIZ) BOKFI

LIZ is a freelance writer living in Simcoe County, Ontario. She is an avid motorcyclist and musician, passions which are often reflected in her articles and song lyrics. She is currently working on a book that will recount some of her most memorable motorcycle adventures. Her website *Roadgypsy.com* offers a more personal glimpse into her biker chick persona.

Recycle Guy

He's the guy you love to hate. Secretly you investigate his activities from behind the kitchen sink window curtain, SOS scrub pad in hand. Your friends talk about him, and in a big *take that!* the family dog urinates over his tracks. How *does* one handle an indignant recycle-truck driver? He leaves behind his mark – the dreaded green sticker: you did not sort your recyclables correctly. Three strikes, you're out – in slippers, two feet of snow, being lectured on how to sort your recyclables. Three green stickers later you shape up, by George. The Recycle Guy has taught you that it's *his* load that gets turned away if waxed juice boxes are mixed with regular cartons. Removal of labels is unnecessary, just caps from plastics. And cardboard is not the same as corrugate. This is serious business.

We are no longer able to avoid recycling. If we mix our recyclables with household garbage, it only increases the number of bags placed curbside. Many municipalities have imposed a bag limit. The result: money spent on extra-bag tags. It's easy to resent the recycle collector.

Your resolve to place the recycle guy *himself* into your chipped and cracked blue box slowly dissolves as he tells of his children getting up late for school. His dog got sprayed by a skunk that morning, so yeah, maybe he *did* pitch your blue bin a little too far into the field. The Recycle Guy has been emptying blue boxes across Canadian counties for years now, yet Canadians continue to resist.

"People don't realize we're human too," he says. "We have families and stress and we *too* get angry at the recycle guy. Take the time to read the recycle guide that comes with your tax bill – it may keep your slippers from getting wet!"

There must have been an awful lot of wet slippers *last* year – this year there are less broken recycle bins; fewer stray bottles in the gutters and The Recycle Guy seems happier. We're sure his children have left for university.

So what about the bigger stuff? Four wheelin' on an ATV along back woods trails definitely gives one a wake up call about garbage disposal.

Carcasses of dead and dying appliances litter both sides of the trail, against the beautiful pine-treed Georgian Bay shoreline. Walking over to check the contents, I slowly lift the lid to an old Kelvinator freezer, afraid of the possibility a dumped carcass of another sort is occupying the inside. I quickly divert my thoughts to the possibility of a briefcase full of cash instead, only to discover sacks of more garbage contained within. The dumpers are lucky they have these hidden trails along which they can dump their cast-offs. Although I greatly have an abhorrence for dumpers, I can somewhat relate to why they are doing the dumping. It costs to have chlorofluorocarbons (Freon) removed; it costs to truck shingles away; garbage collectors don't take building materials. Remember when scrap yards paid *you* for your old car? Now you have to pay *them* to come and take it away so that *they* can collect the money for the metal. So one car doesn't pay much. But, I bet the scrap-truck's tank full of gas would pay for itself in the collection of as many scrap cars it could possibly pick up, in an afternoon of community collection. I may be wrong. I'm just an ordinary, I think "normal" thinking citizen – and from speaking with other residents about this, it appears I do not stand alone on this topic. Maybe the funds from Freon removal and bag tags pay for the county's *No Dumping* signs. They are beautifully crafted, after all. The funds might be more effective buying The Recycle Guy a new safety vest.

How *Not* To Be a Biker *Babe*

Seducing the road. Apparently, the evolution of *Woman* is still evolving.

"Men continually study women, and know nothing about them. Women never study men, and know all about them." (Bob Edwards in *Colombo's Canadian Quotations*, Edited by John Robert Colombo, Hurtig Publishers Edmonton, p. 178)

"Mothers, lock yer daughters up!" Burton Cummings' voice floated across the air, wafting like a subliminal message out of the local hippie-hangout/coffeehouse. The little boy and his sister were hastily herded into the van, the blond-haired boy stumbling over his laces while he continued to stare. The boy's mother, horrified, also continued to stare. I hadn't cleaned my chaps from the bug guts and road dirt since I bought them nine years before. My second pair, actually. I imagined amusingly how they would have appeared now, if the first pair hadn't been stolen from the backpack of my motorcycle. I never did like the look of brand new.

The lines of my black beauty were as smooth and clear as any a beautiful, well-honed machine should have. The sun bounced a golden glow onto her bits, highlighting her beauty even more. This particular day she boasted shades of warm onyx, bathed in a light which would make any man drool at the thought of turning her key...

Her skin was as smooth and clear as any beautiful woman *should* have. Any blemishes that may have been glaringly present were washed away deceptively behind the soft filter of the photographer's lens. Her long blonde hair flowed behind her, seduced into seducing by the precisely aimed fans. The photographer's reflectors bounced a golden glow off her precariously perched-in-the-air buttocks whilst her breasts pushed against the gas tank, creating a dangerously dark cavern which would make any man drool at the thought of losing himself within. But, *does she know where the oil drain plug is located?!* This is the burning question which for years has plagued my biker mind.

Having lived the motorcycle "lifestyle" for many a year, 26 to be exact, the showdown between Biker Chick and Biker *Babe* stilettos a path across my intelligent, road-map-reading brain quite frequently. Despite the growing trend of females entering the sport of motorcycling, still they persist: images of the ideal Biker Babe - the sexy, partially nude girl contorting herself into tantalizing positions simply for the viewing pleasure of the visually stimulated male. She is not discriminatory, gracing motorcycles of every genre: Ms. Motocross; Miss Custom Harley-Davidson. I'd like to see a biker *dude* under similar circumstances – boxer-less, just chaps - minus the beer gut, though. Would men begin to take us seriously if our laundry-room walls were papered with posters of nude, semi-erect-penised men, posing alongside an ironing board, Georgio Armani shirt in hand? The steam button is easier to find than an oil drain plug let me assure you.

Sales of motorcycles to women in Canada sit at close to 30% and are growing. It's apparent women aren't exactly shying away from the male-dominated sport. Women are still in front of the lens – only this time in leather, (jackets, that is) helmets on, posing astride their own machines. No longer content to be the "bitch on the back," women are preferring to be the "bro" in front. Today's biker chicks are not just riding to the corner and back for a Boston Creme either. Increasingly, with bug guts and all, women are choosing to *vacation* by motorcycle, in many instances with like-minded chromosome XX. Female riders are now able to connect with other women through motorcycle groups dedicated to exclusive female membership: Chics N' Chaps, Chrome Divas and Cycle Sisters are just a few of the abundant female motorcycle clubs that have surfaced on the Net. Click *Go,* but Biker Chick beware: evolution of man is just that – evolution of *man,* with more Biker Babes to choose from. Women in motorcycle culture have evolved just enough to jump from custom machines to knobby-tires in one, long-legged full spread. Now hold on to your eggs ladies, I'm on your side. Just type *dirt bike babes* into the search box and it is painfully obvious we biker chicks are in it for the long haul – literally. The only grease you'll find on *our* bodies is that from the road – and from knowing where our oil drain plug is located.

Too slow to crawl out from under the biker babe pin-up poster, and having searched for the reasons only the male-man could understand, I decided to go on the road, in search of real biker chicks - real women. These girls come with no Biker Babe Perfection Warranty.

Tips on How Not To Be a Biker *Babe*

- know the location of your oil drain plug

- save your bikini for the beach

- leave all bug guts and road dirt on your leather chaps

- unless riding around the corner for a Boston Creme, always leave the road dirt under your finger nails

- never attempt to fix your hair after removing your helmet

- *most* importantly, always apply your lip gloss in *your* bike mirror, in full view of the public eye.

Snow-White, And Seven Snow Blowers

Wednesday-night snowfall leaves resident feeling grateful.

Well, it all began with just a few flakes. The crystalline beauties floated through the air like diamonds in the sky, glittering from the glow of streetlights.

By morning, we were drowning in a sea of snow, needing to shovel our way out the door. My best friend, or *woman's* best friend, lifted her paws up and down alternately, a look of disgust on her canine face as she hesitantly descended the front veranda stairs to do her "job."

After donning my snowmobile suit, the real thing, not just those cheap nylon ski pants that absorb water faster than a sponge, I *also* hesitantly descended the *back* veranda to do *my* job. This particular morning, I didn't worry about waking the neighbours with the roar of my snowblower. I saw the evidence, the clues that told me it was okay to chop and grind the white fluffy stuff: footprints, leading from my neighbour's front door to the roadside, where her taxi collects her most mornings. Footprints through a foot and a half of snow, which I'm sure, collected inside the tops of her boots.

As I blew my way out of my back yard, I joined the army of other blowers, all blowing toward a common goal: clearing the way for our vehicles. Occasionally glancing across the way to Mr. G's drive, monitoring his progress as though we were in competition, I noticed the look on his face: disgust. And as shovellers and blowers alike all came walking down the street to help their fellow man (or woman), which included seniors unable to shovel *or* blow, I couldn't help but feel a sense of camaraderie. There we were, seven of us – I actually counted – nameless strangers, working alongside each other, working to clear the mountain of ploughed-in snow from the ends of our driveways.

I remember mornings two years ago, filled with tears during my toils as single parent, getting up at 5:30 a.m. to clear the snow and prepare for my workday. I would curse and grumble my way through the daunting task.

After the storm, I felt jubilant at being able to start my blower and clean up the snow. My muscles burned as I shovelled areas too small for my machine, and I felt high from the endorphin coursing through my veins. High to be alive; high from the accomplishment of shovelling.

You see, one year ago, I struggled just to make it from wheelchair seat onto the seat of a toilet. I couldn't even imagine walking, never mind shovelling snow. A bone tumour had left me in a wheelchair, with an amputated leg, and the after-effects of chemotherapy.

Today, I'm happy to shovel, struggling in my prosthetic but happy to help my struggling neighbours in their time of need - and happy to be alive. Snow, glorious snow. As long as I am able to roar to life, along with my blower, let it snow, let it snow, let it snow.

GEORGE BELAJAC

GEORGE is a retired school teacher living in Orillia with his wife, Elizabeth. His enthusiasm for writing has resulted in his poetry being published in anthologies such as *Island Skies, Shadows of the Dawn* and *A Golden Morning.* He has completed a juvenile novel, a series of rhyming stories for children and several short stories.

As an ongoing member of the Mariposa Writers' Group, he has shared in the annual Lake Country Literary Lapses Festival at the Leacock Museum both as a runner-up in the Poetry Contest and a participant in the various events of this Festival.

George's inspirations stem from personal experiences. His children, grandchildren and former students frequently become the focal point of his writing.

Walking to Work

This morning, he decided to walk the 35 minutes to work. For some reason, he seemed to have a certain alertness or mind focus that he had not had for a long time. Such compelling thoughts had to be initiated by another source or inspiration, way beyond his aptitude.

"To forestall the inevitable would simply preclude the notion that all things at one time or other come to an end.

"Furthermore, meeting up with chance would only afford a pre-determined degree of success.

"But patience, the indubitable virtue and wisdom the wily general can eliminate false hopes and aspirations that may undermine one's decision-making process."

Unbelievable! Such weird notions coming from him?

Hardly likely! His pace quickened as he rounded the corner.

The greed factor that was seething and ready to inflict its venom cowered in the shades of the morning sunlight. He took two steps to his left and deftly dropped a toonie into the panhandler's cup. He knew the beggar would be there. He was there every day. Too often he drove past, since he seldom ventured to walk. But, nevertheless, he noticed him all the time, sitting in the same place – sunglasses, baseball cap and dark beard shielding his face.

A few more steps and a quick glance back showed the panhandler now basking in the rays of the morning sunlight.

A faint smile emerged on his face as he continued toward the office. A charitable donation given to him? Why? Where was all this coming from? He'd never before given a cent, let alone a toonie, to this person. What was a toonie in the scheme of things? After all, hundreds and thousands of toonies had left his pockets and accounts in the past few weeks. This was the outcome of driving a different route and certainly not one which took him home from work. As of late, he had spent many afternoons and early evenings whiling away the hours consumed by a passion, a passion to win at all costs! There was even discreetness and lies in this risky pursuit that took him to the outskirts of town. He alone was responsible for this 'impassioned craze' that took him to Casino Rio. He didn't want to be seen, welcomed or acknowledged by anyone. The less conspicuous the better. He only wanted to fulfill this insatiable urge and to relish alone in his dreams of victory over a combatant that simply refused to surrender to his persistent onslaught. He knew he was in for a desperate fight. But, all of his previous knowledge, common sense and determination to avoid the pitfalls of gambling meant nothing to him now. Whatever he had or whatever it took to gain 'a high' he would unwittingly do - he wanted it all!

With this in mind, he ventured away from the crowds to relish in the more-subdued or less-frequented areas of the Rio. When others crowded into the same area or even sat beside him, his grimacing look surfaced. He hated this, but rather than move, he felt it wiser to wait until they moved. And often enough they did! Perhaps a simple glance at him infringed on their fun. With his glazed look, he quickly forged on as minutes passed into hours. The impact of the constant noise, the flashing lights of the slots and the unceasing drone of the Casino melted away into his quagmire of thoughts. His arched back remained rigid as he leaned closer to the slot. He was immersed in a world a million miles away. Little did he know when he entered Casino Rio that finding solace there would prove to be a nightmare.

The death of Sara may have had a more profound effect on him than one might expect and, what the heck, he needed something to take his mind off her tragic and sudden death. Casino Rio was open 24-7!

From the first day, he found a certain serenity he was looking for and on that day when a smiling cashier came to reward him with his winnings, everything else seemed to be forgotten. As the days and weeks wore on, the serene feeling became an uncontrollable urge to play on and on.

Even fatigue and boredom could not stop him. Any winnings, that infrequently occurred, were poured back into the machines and the losses continued to mount! Worst of all, he couldn't understand why. His passion to win was happening, but at a very high cost. It was no longer about him! He was acting like a zombie to those around him and now he was a liar. He lied to his wife about overtime hours at work. He lied about missing funds from savings accounts. His attitude and performance were not going unnoticed, especially after his wife had contacted management. Co-workers witnessing his decisions and work ethic asked if everything at home was all right. His closest friends were indeed correct in sensing that Sara's death had brought on a change in his personality. He seemed to be avoiding not only those around him, but also those closest to him. He now felt trapped and was suffocating under the pressure. Lies, a lack of friends and what seemed like close scrutiny by his wife and co-workers were causing his mind to race. But today something had come over him that he had never felt before. In the next few steps his mind suddenly flashed back to the previous early evening. Once more he glanced back but this time he saw an immediate vision of the silver-haired lady he had met at the Rio. She came and sat at the slot next to his. She was undoubtedly a senior and more than likely a grandmother although she never said she was. Her clear image and words must have touched his heart more than he would ever admit. It was almost as if he knew her. He poured out the details of Sara's tragic death and how he felt he may have been responsible. He knew the Rio was a one-way ticket to his personal destruction and he was now out of control. As the silver-haired lady turned to him and took his hands, there seemed to be an underlying sense of urgency in her eloquent yet serious words. She assured him that any guilt he may have felt was forgiven and that those around him loved him and understood the heaviness in his heart.

Were these weird notions and thoughts coming from her?

The coffee shop was only a few steps away and today he would pick up coffee and donuts for the staff. At 8:30 a.m. he would phone his wife.

And tomorrow he would again be 'walking to work'!

Ghosts Long Past

There he is on that park bench - over by the walkway
Seems free from worry
He's pulling his faded ball cap over his eyes
Must be he's preparing for blissful solitude
To dream only of good times
For the ghosts once lived are long past
His warm woolen hooded sweater is a perfect pillow
On the curved arm of the bench
His scruff of beard and ponytail tied tightly
With a shortened black shoelace
Accentuate the plaid lumber jacket
And tattered blue jeans
Unexpectedly, his right hand thrusts upward
As if to hold some meaning
Then slowly it descends
To tuck itself into the warmth of his pocket
Seems ready to revel in his dream
That takes him to his paradise
For the ghosts are long past
But he'll not linger
The chill stiffens his face
Odessa's sharp talons now gently grip his shoulder
Bearing watch – she awaits his stirring
A wisp of cloud filters the sunlight
Beckoning his hand to inch further into the folds of his pocket
To grasp her reward
This journey's been precluded
Odessa lifts – then dives
Directing him to nourish his hunger
For he once gave her life
So he sits in shabby attire – to taste

One hand thrusts upward then slowly descends
Alas, a smile imbues his being
Odessa soars – far and away
And the ghosts are long past.

The Concert

I, with my knapsack
A wayfaring lad
Upon entry – a dubious freak
Oblivious to the gathering crowd

But with the power of might
To witness this testament
Such divine providence
Has not befallen me till now

A concert so grand
Magic distilled
"A once in a lifetime performance."
Yet, for only a select few?
Pray tell, not to be!

The whisper of the music
Moods the selection
Softly – ever so softly

An angel's voice renders itself
A celestial assembly emerges
Stillness in the air
Hearts pause to quiet
Hands gently touch – moulding into one
Jupiter gazes in adulation
Ninatta serenely appraises
A tear reaches down from the depths of one's soul
To betray the joy of these precious moments

Entranced in a dream
Memories surge
Oh, such lyrics – to beguile my thoughts
The music crescendos in startling symmetry

She smiles
Her arms wrap in splendour
To hold me to her heart
And I, but a wayfaring lad
Am charged to feel life!
Perhaps, never to love like this again.

A Solemn Oath

None had e'er faced such wrath of the sea
For these prisoners of the main knew no fear
But the eye of the hurricane near upon them now
Gave visions of hell and thoughts unclear

"Take up the strain wayward curs
Pull with all y'ur might
For a moment wasted is a moment lost
Lest you choose to face a ghostly sight."

"I'm with you, master, but my hands can't grip
My strength has ebbed away
Yet, a moment measured to unshackle these chains
Then perchance, I might see another day."

"Your foolish whining shall not be answered
Filthy dogs, you'll serve your time
Now gather your brawn and cry out no more
For the depths of these waters may not be sublime."

"But master, he pleads with honesty for all
Alas, free us now to challenge this watery foe
We will gather our force with untiring zeal
'Aye master', we pledge, as these gale winds blow."

"Stinking pigs, I will not adhere to your pitiful plight
Nor relent to your desperate plea
But my conscience now unveils a sordid guilt
Should 'I' be lost at sea."

"Then waste no time to meditate
For Hades cries out for our wretched souls
Release us now for the water spills
Bear witness not to the burning coals."

"If I could trust you, one and all
To swear a solemn oath of revival
Then no blame shall befall my generous soul
Should the hand of fate deny our survival."

"Dear master, your grace will never be denied
Let the devil consume his sorrow
Your deed shall absolve all feeling of guilt
Should any survive the morrow."

SARAH N. THOMPSON

SARAH is the youngest member of the Mariposa Writers Group. Her interest in writing started about the time she learned the alphabet. She was continuously read to as a child and decided, before she could even write a full sentence, that she would be a writer one day. She wrote her first novel in the third grade and began writing poetry in grade four.

Although she hasn't had anything published yet, she hopes this will happen in the next few years. In addition to poems and short stories, Sarah enjoys writing opinion pieces. One of her writing traits, regrettably, is that she begins novels and never finishes them, because by the time she's finished the first chapter, she has five other ideas about it. Eventually, she is certain she will finish one and it will be published.

Sarah also wants to challenge herself by trying different types of writing, such as newspaper articles, which she's just getting good at. Without constantly writing, Sarah says she wouldn't know what to do. She usually writes when she's bored, angry, lonely or when someone hands her a math test. Sarah lives in Orillia with her family.

Wolves

Pinpricks of light surrounded the earth, like fireflies in the distance or flickering souls above the rain-drenched land. An orb hung suspended in the night. It shone brightly, enchanting the hunter who howled longingly, lusting for an unseen reality. Her paw steps were silent, her hot breath coming in puffs of steam through the crisp fall air. She paused a minute, pricking up her ears. The distant howl of a male answered her from far away. She called back to him.

No, he seemed to say, *you come here.* She turned away, loping back up the mountain to her den. She couldn't leave her precious home, not now, not even for her mate. She felt the stirring of life in her belly and settled in for the night. Let him bring the meat to her, she thought.

An old she-wolf greeted her at the entrance to their rock cave. Beneath a ripped and matted coat, strength flowed through her body and wisdom lit her golden eyes. She dipped her head respectfully to her young daughter, careful not to make eye contact. Then she left, as silently as her companion had entered, to blend in with the shadows.

Padding farther up towards the peak of the mountain, she looked on with fond memories at the place she had called home since birth. She had raised her three pups there, hunted with the skill and speed of a pack and howled secrets to the wind. She had felt joy, love and even sorrow. Never had she imagined that their home would not last forever, never had she known that her daughter's pups would be born to die. The blissful ignorance of the wild had been her blanket. It had kept the balance of her world. Only a hunter greater than herself could tip that balance, one whose heart was blackened with greed and whose power was endless. Standing so high above the world, she knew naught of what was to come, but as the moon and the stars faded from the sky and a pale light crept slowly toward the wolves, only time hung between them and their fate.

BARBARA STREET BRECHIN

BARBARA lives on Brechinbrae Farm in Oro/Medonte Township, Ontario. She spent most of her 30-year teaching career in Orillia. Her first travel experiences lay within Canada but, within five years, she had expanded her horizons to include such destinations as: South America, India, China, and Africa. By 1985, Barbara was becoming a travel addict and eagerly seized an opportunity to opt for early retirement. This allowed her to incorporate Connoisseur Travelplan Enterprises - a company which would allow her to organize and escort group trips. However, it was her own personal travel which would provide fodder for her writing. Barbara's Peru Diaries inspired her first historical novel, *The Diaz Crystal*, while the story she has chosen for this Anthology is based on her India Diaries, specifically her trip to Dharamsala and New Delhi.

Seeking the Dalai Lama

Most people recognize that among world leaders there is no one like His Holiness the Dalai Lama, religious and secular leader of Tibet. He has been travelling the world since 1999 in an attempt to further the cause of a Free Tibet. In 1989 he became a Nobel Peace Prize laureate. Exiled from Tibet, the Dalai Lama lives in solitude in the Dharamsala region of Northern India. Here in the Himalayan foothills, he is surrounded by scenery reminiscent of Tibet.

Since my trip to Tibet a number of years ago, my interest in the spiritual leader of its people had been growing, and in 1992 my friend Laura and I set out to seek a private audience with His Holiness in India. On our arrival in New Delhi, we were disappointed to read in the newspaper that the Dalai Lama would be in Dharamsala during our five- day stay there. Our short stay did not allow us to visit the magnificent Cathedral and Monastery located outside the gates of the Dalai Lama's private residence, but pictures prove what the determination and resilience of a gentle people can accomplish – albeit in exile from their beloved homeland.

Before we left Dharamsala, the manager of our hotel learned from official sources that the Dalai Lama would possibly be in New Delhi during our stay there. He agreed to write a letter of introduction to be presented to the secretary for all arrangements in Delhi. As fate would have it our flight from Dharamsala was canceled owing to monsoon rains, so on the following day, we embarked on a terrifying 12-hour taxi ride to New Delhi.

Our descent from the mountains lay over narrow, steep switchbacks strewn with rock slides and wet from the rains. I held onto a strap on the side of the van; braced myself with my left hand on the seat ahead of me; and prayed we would make it. By the time we reached the Punjab the traffic was horrendous. Neither of us cared to comment on the horrible accidents – overturned trucks, transport trailers, buses (14 in all), a gas truck which was totally burned, a white van spattered with blood and a dead horse lying on the highway. However, all things good or bad do come to an end and we arrived in New Delhi in 120 degree C. temperature, hot, thirsty and totally exhausted but grateful to have made it.

Fortunately, Laura had a good friend in New Delhi whose husband was a Lieutenant General in the Indian Army. He agreed to take us to Tibet House and off we went to try our luck there. The contact at Tibet House was very agreeable; looked at my book of Tibetan photos; listened to our story and advised us to go the Dalai Lama's office. So back out into the insufferable heat. We were lucky to have a private chauffeur and did not have to depend on cab service. At the office we were again greeted by a very amiable gentleman. Again I presented by gift of photos for his Holiness and requested that we be granted a private audience. From the look on Dorje's face, I realized we were not going to receive good news. "So sorry, so very sorry," he said, "tomorrow is the biggest holiday of the year in India, the celebration of Independence Day. All stores will be closed and the streets awash with crowds of people. The Dalai Lama's flight is not expected until about 3 p.m. and, with all that traffic…Laura and I must have looked heavy-hearted and we certainly were that. Our overnight train to Jaisalmer for our camel safari would depart Delhi station at 6.30 p.m. Even if we were granted an audience it would have to occur by 4.30 or we would never make it to the train station. I suggested it might be best for me to leave the book of photos with Dorje. Apparently this triggered his sympathy for he said, "it seems such a pity that you came all this way from Canada to see the Dalai Lama only to be disappointed! Keep the pictures with you and I will see what I can do. I'll call you at the Imperial Hotel if I have any success."

Back at our hotel, Laura went for a swim and I lay down, totally exhausted. I slept until our phone rang at 3. It was Dorje! I was so excited I almost dropped the phone. "Yes, you have your private audience at 4.45 but you must be at the Oshaka Hotel by 4.30."

If you had been at the Oshaka Hotel on the afternoon of August 15, you would have found two very nervous Canadians bearing cameras, gifts and the traditional white silk khatas (ceremonial scarves) to present to Tenzin Gyastso, the fourteenth Dalai Lama of Tibet. Although our meeting was scheduled for 4.45, we had arrived early and sat impatiently in the lobby. At 4.45 we had still not been summoned and we grew apprehensive. Had we come all this way, crossed so many hurdles only to be met with yet another disappointment? Laura went to reception to inquire and to show the liaison officer's business card we had been given in Dharmasala. It worked. Moments later, we were escorted to a small waiting room on the third floor. The Dalai Lama was late arriving, and several other audiences were backed up – but we were next!

Our friend Doje came to offer instructions on the Tibetan way of presenting the ceremonial khatas. However, in less than a minute, another gentleman arrived to say we must come quickly. His Holiness was waiting for us. Our cameras and bags were inspected and we were ushered into a beautifully decorated reception room. Bouquets of red roses were set out on white marble tables; a huge elephant, painted black, red and gold, was positioned in a corner near the brocaded divan where the Dalai Lama was sitting. Rising, the Dalai Lama walked toward me. He was wearing the traditional maroon over saffron monk's robes and his olive tinted glasses but it was his smile, his warmth, his aura that lit up the room. I put the binder of photos on a table and began the presentation of the khata. Gone were any of Dorje's instructions! I just bowed, utter the traditional "Namaste" and said, "Your Holiness, this is such a great joy!"

Once again I was amazed by his smile as he placed the silk scarf around my neck and asked me to be seated in a chair next to him. I had read that the Dalai Lama always endeavours to engage his visitors in a warm personal exchange and here I was experiencing that very thing. The photos I presented him with were all taken during my 1985 trip to Tibet. He turned each page and made numerous comments. At the one of me in an Indian sari, he chuckled and said "Indian!" Another was of our Tibetan guide. At this point he spoke to his aides asking, "How would he learn English?" At a picture of a small boy in a military hat, I again hear his wonderful giggle as he pointed at the child. I had a beautiful little picture of an alcove in the Potala Palace which I was unable to resist pointing out. His comment "No! No! Not Potala!"

Potala was Tenzin Gyatso's home from the time he was a very small boy. He ascended the throne at age six and spent every winter there until his escape in 1959. He would surely know every inch of that palace. In my embarrassment, I hastily added, "I must be mistaken, Sir." Now I ask you, why would I have addressed a humble man who wants to be known as simple a Buddhist monk, Sir?

When Laura asked for permission to take a picture of me with him, one of his attendees announced that the Dalai Lama loves to have his picture taken. This was accomplished and then it was Laura's turn. She then asked if we could we could both pose for another photo with him. We sat on either side of this dynamic public figure; he closed his right hand around my left and his left around Laura's right. You could feel the amazing energy flowing from him to us. What a marvelous experience that was! He then asked for two copies of one of his books to be brought to him. He signed each book, then pointed out the Tibetan words above his signature saying, "That's a prayer."

It was over then. Two highly elated Canadians had enjoyed a private audience with Dalai Lama of Tibet. All we had to do now as get back to our hotel, pick up our bags and arrive at the station in time for the six o'clock train to Jaisalmer in order to begin our camel safari in Rajasthan. Did we make it? That's another story for another time.

ANNE O'ROURKE

ANNE was born in Germany. Her training as a dress designer there provided her with the necessary qualifications to teach pattern drafting at Seneca College in Toronto. Anne is now retired and living in Moonstone where she writes poetry of day-to-day events that occur in her life. She volunteers to help persons with disabilities and heart and stroke survivors in Orillia. Anne also plays the accordion for the Black Forest Singers in Barrie and hikes, bikes and canoes with the Ganaraska Hiking Club.

The Life and Afterlife of the Turkey Vulture

My good friend, Pat, retired as a teacher from the College of Art in Toronto and bought an old United Church in Hillsdale. She converted the basement into her living quarters which in wintertime is dark and gloomy. With the first warmth of spring she moves to her spare bed up on the altar in the church. Here the sun shines through the beautiful stained glass windows and here she enjoys her music and the acoustics of the church. On the foot of the bed is a huge stuffed turkey vulture. (How she got it would make another story.) Pat is also a great gardener and has two fishponds behind the church. One day she phones me in panic because a heron had eaten some of the fish. "What can I do now?" The next day she found the solution - " If I would take the stuffed turkey vulture and stand him at the edge of the pool, but move him every hour so the heron believes that the vulture is real" --etc. etc. So I wrote:

Once he was proud
Soaring high in the air
Over lakes, over hills
He was free.
He swooped down on road kill
Or mice or moles,
Took them up to his nest in the tree.
This all came to an end and his life was cut short
and we do not know how he died.
Was he caught in a trap?
Or chased by a dog?
Or hit by a bullet in flight?
And now comes Phase II
He is still in demand
As a stuffed bird he is guarding Pat.
His claws they are sharp
And his eyes they are fierce
As he stares all night at her bed.

With a vulture like this

I am not surprised that he keeps all the Lovers away.

Who would dare to come near

Even though she tries hard to find

Someone to roll in the hay ~~with~~.

And now comes Phase III

And he has a new job

To look "real" by the side of the pool.

He waits for the Heron

Who for sure will come back for more fish - and he is no fool.

So don't think it's the end

After you die,

They could stuff you

And make you look real.

They could find you a job

In a store or a bank

Wouldn't this have a lot of appeal?

The Fish Pond

The fish pond is dirty so let's clean it up.
We take all the fish out and give it a scrub.
So he bought a kids' pool, brought it back to his house,
And he nearly fainted blowing it up with his mouth.
Then he went on his knees and started the fun.
He had to catch thirty fish, one by one,
By then it was evening and he needed a rest.
No more fish or fish pond - he did his best.
The smart wife, who is also known as fish lover,
Put over the kids' pool a big plastic cover,
Early next morning she jumped out of bed,
To check how the fish are: what a shock she had.
A clan of raccoons must have come through the night.
They ate every fish while the house was all quiet.
They only left some bones, and what was not nice,
All over the backyard were sixty fish eyes.
The moral of the story: keep your pond not too clean,
The fish do not mind if it's slimy and green.

The Midnight Garbage Dumper

Who driveth so late through the night and wind?
It is the garbage dumper.
His truck overflows with all kinds of stuff
But he knows not to drop his junk there.
He drives through the forest and checks out the lanes
And now he turns off the light.
He turns off the motor and starts to unload.
The forest around him is quiet.
He throws out some tires,
Old pots and some wires,
A green chesterfield full of holes,
An old kitchen sink,
And a doll dressed in pink
And parts of a tent without poles.
Next morning we hike
And the sun is so bright,
But the mess in the woods spoils the walk.
What happened that night?
The trees see it all.
They would tell us if they could just talk.